To the Heights

*A Novel Based on the Life of
Blessed Pier Giorgio Frassati*

To the Heights

A Novel Based on the Life of
Blessed Pier Giorgio Frassati

BRIAN KENNELLY

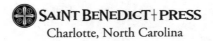

SAINT BENEDICT✝PRESS
Charlotte, North Carolina

Cataloging-in-Publication data on file with the Library of Congress.

Cover artwork copyright © Chris Pelicano.

ISBN: 978-1-61890-632-8

Published in the United States by
Saint Benedict Press, LLC
PO Box 269
Gastonia, NC 28053
www.SaintBenedictPress.com

Printed in India

Contents

Prologue

When Saint Benedict Press approached me about this project, my immediate reaction was one of hesitation. How do you tell the story of a real-life, historical figure, especially one as holy as Pier Giorgio Frassati? How do you do him justice and display his virtues accurately? How do you take what biographical information we have and weave it together, while doing your best to fill in the gaps of what we don't know? How do you speak for a man on the path to Sainthood, a man revered by Popes?

These troubling questions kept me awake for nearly a week. Luckily, I had a newborn baby to keep me company on those sleepless nights.

But above these issues was a dilemma trumping them all—the opposing option was far worse. To decline the offer meant forfeiting an amazing opportunity. Could I let such a chance pass me by, to not only learn more about Pier Giorgio Frassati myself, but also bring him to thousands of others? As with many matters throughout our lives, clarity came through prayer, and here I am writing this just over a year later.

The burden of sitting down to write a biography is certainly a difficult one, but to write a historical fiction novel bleeds over into something else. There are different

challenges, different rules, and even more people scrutiniz-
ing your work. A writer opens himself up to criticism with
each word he writes, a truth only exaggerated when writing
about a historical figure.

So why embark on such a project? Why not just write
a biography?

There is certainly a place for biographies in the librar-
ies and bookshelves of our world, especially of the Saints.
They are informative, inspirational, and integral to spreading the Faith. But most are not told through the medium of
a story, and there is nothing more powerful than this; one
need only look to the greatest Teacher we've ever known,
who chose to teach in parables.

There is no denying biographies have the ability to
teach us many things about the colossal figures of our past,
lessons we may even be able to apply to our own lives. But
does it have the ability to make us cry the way a story can?
Does it journey into the caverns of our soul, where the
deepest truths hide, and bring those truths back to the
surface?

I have always felt that reading a biography, or any
non-fiction book, is like looking through a pair of binoculars, while reading fiction is like looking through a kaleidoscope. In both cases you're presenting something new
to your senses, but the binoculars merely draw you closer
to a reality that is a distant part of *this* world, while the
kaleidoscope draws you closer to the possible realities of the
world beyond, where lights and colors dazzle in such a way
we are not accustomed to here on earth. The beauty of historical fiction is that it combines the two, so that perhaps

you're looking through the lens of a telescope at the glittering lights of the cosmos, helping you to make sense of your humble place in the universe. But beyond any poetic analogy that can be made, the truth is that when you fall into a story, your own story begins to have more meaning.

It's my hope that in relaying the life of a young man like Pier Giorgio Frassati through the prism of a story, we can come to know him better than we would in the pages of a biography, or even a book of his own letters. We can place ourselves in his shoes, relate to him, and view life through his eyes. His experiences become *our* experiences, and he holds our hand as we learn from them.

But the reader must not forget that this is a fictional novel. Artistic liberties had to be taken to fill in the day-to-day details of Pier Giorgio's life. Much of what we know about him comes from the many letters he wrote to family and friends. But a novel about a young man sitting down to pen dozens of letters simply would not work. Therefore, it was necessary, at times, to make reasonable conjectures, both to connect the dots of his life and to ensure the story flows in an engaging and compelling fashion. I've taken the facts, letters, and verifiable episodes from his life and blended them together into what I hope is a story that will give the reader a chance to know Pier Giorgio in a whole new light.

Throughout the course of my research, I began to see just how important Pier Giorgio was, and how vital it was that his narrative spread to the masses. He devoted much of his life to works of charity, spending a great deal of time in the ghettos of Turin with the poor and sick, and was an avid believer in the importance of the sacraments and devotion to Our Lady.

But beyond his spiritual life, he was a good-looking, charismatic, and popular young man who loved to disappear in the rugged Alps of Northern Italy, climbing toward the heights and above the clouds. He had dozens of friends, girls loved him, and he possessed an eternal zest and optimistic attitude in everything he did. To use a modern term, he was simply "cool." There is a quote attributed to Pope St. John Paul II where he claims that the Church needs saints who wear jeans and sneakers instead of veils and cassocks, and saints who eat pizza and go to the movies. If our late Holy Father truly said this, he needn't look further than to this young Italian.

Pier Giorgio was also bold enough to get his hands dirty when he spoke out passionately against the evils of Fascism, even coming to blows with Mussolini's thugs on numerous occasions. But perhaps most fascinating of all, he carried a unique cross in the form of high-society parents who actually frowned upon his intense love of the Catholic Church, doing their best to steer him away from his religious practices and charitable work.

In short, Pier Giorgio is perhaps one of the most unique and fascinating souls to ever journey down the path to Sainthood, a man John Paul II called, "a man of the Beatitudes." But the power of his story is frozen solid in an immense glacier sitting atop the globe; my goal is to melt that glacier, letting his life seep into the oceans and fall upon each shore in the form of virtuous waves that tumble and crash with an Italian accent.

I was only 29 when I began writing this, so it was rather fitting and providential to study a man so inspirational to young people in particular. When I neared the completion of this book, I felt as if Pier Giorgio had become my brother. It is my hope and prayer that you feel the same way after reading it. Through all my research and writing efforts, consisting of long hours in the quiet pitch of night, I have tried to relay his tale with the utmost respect and honor. For any failures, may God forgive me.

My thanks goes out to the people of Saint Benedict Press and TAN Books, especially Rick Rotondi and Conor Gallagher, for presenting me with this opportunity. I also want to thank Allison Schumacher, Paul Thigpen, and Morgan Witt for all their help and edits. On a personal note, I want to thank my parents, as well as my brother and his family, and my wife's family, for their continued love and support. Last but not least, I must thank my wife, Tina (you're my favorite person), and our children, Connor and Magdalene.

Blessed Pier Giorgio Frassati, pray for us.

1

A Rose in Return

Antonio cupped his two hands together, locking them with his knuckles.

"Place your foot here, Paolo, and I'll lift you up."

"How will you get out with no one to lift *you* up?" the younger boy asked.

"I'm tall enough to reach the ledge and pull myself up. I'll be right behind you."

"Are you sure we should do this? We could get in trouble."

"We convinced Mother Vanzetti we were sick with our coughing. You heard her; she told us to stay in bed and not get out for the rest of the day, so that we don't get the others sick. She won't come down to check on us, I promise. And anyway, it's worth the risk. Think of all the times he came to visit us. Now, we'll repay him with a visit."

"But he has died. How will he know?"

"Trust me, Paolo, he'll know we're there."

Paolo glanced up at the window. It led out of the basement of the Provincial Institute for Children and came out at the curb of Corso Giovanni Lanza. He heard

1

the swooshing of cars driving by.

"Is it locked?"

"No, just flip the latch and it will pop open. You already asked this. Stop with all your reasons to not do this."

Paolo took a deep breath and placed his bare foot inside Antonio's hands. His older friend lifted and balanced him before the window, long enough for him to flip the latch. He pushed it open and squeezed his body through the narrow, rectangular window, climbing out onto the bustling street. A moment later, Paolo saw Antonio's hands clasp the edge of the windowsill. He grunted as he struggled to pull himself up, scratching his feet against the inside wall to gain leverage. When Antonio had joined Paolo on the street, they smiled and snuck off around the corner of the block.

The closer they got to the Church of La Crocetta, the thicker the crowd grew. They appeared unassumingly from each alley that formed the gridded blocks of the city, gathering like a flock of birds from the wooded forests for their winter migration. The church acted as a magnet, drawing in the crowds from all over Turin.

Normally, two barefooted orphans, dressed in rags and a week removed from a bath, might draw the ire of those passing by. But this crowd was different—it was filled with the poor, the lonely, the sick, the degenerate. They were the broken of the city, the castaways of the gutter, all gathering to take witness to the procession without concern of two orphans joining them.

The boys stopped at the edge of the crowd a hundred yards from the church.

"Come on," Antonio said, grabbing Paolo's hand, "we can get closer."

"Wait. . . ."

Paolo ripped his hand away and ran across the street.

"Paolo! Where are you going? Paolo!"

Antonio watched his young friend slither through the sea of people to a flower vendor across the street. Paolo slipped up to the right side of the wooden cart, waiting for the merchant's attention to be drawn in the other direction. When the man's eyes slid away, distracted by a young, brunette woman, Paolo plucked a red rose from a bouquet and sprinted back across the street.

"He'd bring us flowers when he visited; I'd like to give him a rose in return."

Antonio nodded and smiled, then grabbed Paolo's hand and together they snaked their way through the crowd. They fell to all fours and crawled across the concrete and in between the legs of unknowing adults. After a few minutes, they arrived at the edge of a group of policemen holding back the throngs of people. Beyond them sat the church, with its dark brick bell tower rising up against the summer sky.

"What now?" Paolo asked.

"Now, we wait. The procession should be arriving soon. I heard a man say they had to come down Via Marco Polo because the crowd following the casket numbered too many for the other roads."

Paolo nodded and glanced at the people surrounding them. They were all giants, hovering two feet above him. Normally he might be intimidated by such an assembly of adults, but an unexplainable peace hung over the busy streets and quelled his fears. There was a common sadness that united them all and brought a calming presence to each person. A woman to his right cried into the shoulder of her husband. A man to his left also had eyes glistening wet with tears.

It was a strange feeling, the boy thought, to be among so many people but somehow feel connected to them all, a connection brought to them through one young man, a man who had visited he, Antonio, and all the other orphans dozens of times over the last several years. A smile came to Paolo as he recalled his dark-haired friend and all the times he had played games with the children.

"So many people," he remarked to Antonio, "and they're all so sad. Did they know him like we did?"

Antonio looked in all directions, surveying the faces from below. He nodded. "I'm sure they did, or they wouldn't be here."

"How did he know them all so well?"

"I don't know, Paolo. He always made me feel like I was the only person in the world he wanted to speak with."

"I felt the same."

"I suppose he did this for all these people, too."

"But I want to know. I want to know how he did this, so I can be like him."

"I'd like to know, too. But I think one day we will, Paolo. One day we'll *all* know his story."

A murmur rose from within the crowd like a wave rippling in the sea. Heads turned and peered down the street. A procession of men in dark suits with a brown casket hovering atop their shoulders came into view on the horizon's edge.

"Get your rose ready," Antonio said, putting his arm around Paolo. "Here comes Pier Giorgio."

2
A Simple Gift

Pier Giorgio sat at his desk drawing a picture, his short legs dangling above the floor. His head remained steady, perched and still as if turned to stone, but his eyes darted up and down as he surveyed in the distance the bell tower of the Church of La Crocetta.

It rose up in clear view from his bedroom window, the white clock and the bells above it, all framed by the tower made of a dark and rich-colored brick. He tried in vain to duplicate what his eyes saw across the block to the paper resting on his desk, but nothing met with his approval. He crumpled up his latest effort and hurled it toward the garbage pail in the corner of the room, which sat overflowing with dozens of such balls of paper.

"I'll never be able to draw it," he yelled at himself.

In the hollows of his despair, for no reason he could fathom, he thought of his grandmother, Linda Ametis. Perhaps, he wondered, she found her way into the recesses of his juvenile thoughts because she was such an avid visitor to The Church of La Crocetta on her visits with the family. She had traveled up from her town of Alassio on

7

the Mediterranean. Pier Giorgio had been to visit her last summer and each day they would go searching for wild-flowers growing in the fields behind her villa. He recalled how much she had enjoyed this.

"I need a break," he admitted.

He ran downstairs and found his grandmother in the family's living room. She sat reading a book in the light of a window overlooking the Piazza d'Armi.

"Grandmother Ametis, come outside with me to pick flowers."

"Oh, dear boy," she said, placing her book in her lap and caressing his cherub face. Her wrinkled hands felt rough against his smooth cheeks. "You're so sweet, but I'm tired today. Perhaps you may go in search of flowers with-out me and bring them back so I can see."

Pier Giorgio thought for a moment before smiling and kissing her cheek. "I'll bring you a bouquet!"

He sprinted out of the house, leaving the sound of his grandmother's laughter behind and entering the streets of his hometown. Turin sat nestled at the base of the Alps in Northern Italy, some 400 miles from Rome. It was a majes-tic city with a romantic skyline and a picturesque expanse of snow-capped mountains surrounding it. Cathedrals, castles, villas, and other architectural gems dating back sev-eral centuries filled each block, as common as lamps in a house and just as overlooked if one did not stop to appre-ciate the splendor.

Knowing his parents would not let their six-year old son venture far, Pier Giorgio scanned the nearby area of Crocetta. He plucked and gathered flowers from a bed surrounding a fountain, filling his hands like a bride on her wedding day.

On his way back home he turned a corner too quickly, running directly into a woman who, coincidentally enough, also held a bouquet of flowers. He fell to the ground as she stumbled back. Both of them dropped everything they held.

"Oh my, where are you going in such a hurry, little one?"

She crouched down to help him up.

"I'm sorry, Signora," he replied, dusting himself off. "I was running home to give my grandmother these flowers."

"What a nice boy you are! Well, let's pick these up so you can get home to her."

The two of them began to gather the flowers sprawled on the sidewalk. Pier Giorgio glanced up at her black dress and the dark veil blanketing her hair.

"Where were you going with all these flowers, Sister?"

"Oh, I'm no Sister. I am a simple woman going to place a bouquet in the chapel at La Crocetta. I have just come from the nursery. Well, alright then," she said, seeing that they had both collected all their flowers, "run home to your grandmother."

She moved around Pier Giorgio but after several steps he called after her. "Sister?"

She turned. "I told you, boy, I'm not a nun."

"Sister, won't you give one of these to Jesus for me? My grandmother loves him; I don't think she'll mind."

He separated one of his daffodils and held it out to her. She smiled and came back to him, taking it from his hand.

"I'll be sure to deliver it to him."

"Thank you, Sister!"

She chuckled and rubbed his head. "You don't listen so well, but I think one day you'll see that Jesus will make you a saint."

Pier Giorgio shrugged before turning and running down the street, not stopping until he had laid his flowers in the lap of his beloved grandmother.

3

A Child's Compassion

Although the Frassati family called Turin home, their hearts resided in Pollone, a quaint town fifty miles to the north where Pier Giorgio's family owned a vacation villa. The grand, two-story home had been in his mother's family for years and was often where Grandmother and Grandfather Ametis could be found hiding from the world.

The speed of life slowed within the confines of Pollone, earning it the appropriate nickname, "Peaceful Pollone" from the family. It was here where Pier Giorgio created some of his fondest childhood memories, no doubt because it meant much time spent with his grandparents. Their presence, combined with the serenity of the secluded town, calmed the normal hustle associated with everyday life in Turin.

"Are you ready to go?" Grandfather Ametis called up the stairs to Pier Giorgio.

"I'm coming!" came the young boy's reply. He ran across the upstairs hall, his rapid footsteps echoing throughout the house, and descended the stairs. His grandfather smiled and rubbed his head. "Do you have the food?" Pier Giorgio asked.

"Of course! It's by the door. Let's go, or we'll be late."

Together they set out on foot to the nearby daycare center, an "asilo," as it was known.

"Do you know these children we're delivering the food to?" Pier Giorgio asked as they meandered down the narrow and winding roads to the town of Pollone.

"I don't know them personally, but I know many of the Sisters who watch after them."

"Why don't they have food to eat?"

"Well, their families don't have the means that our family is blessed to have. Their parents send them to the *asilo* so they'll be given proper care and attention."

"I'm glad we have this leftover food from the dinner party, then."

Grandfather Ametis smiled.

They walked further, through the town and across the river to where the daycare center rested before the rolling hills. Inside, Pier Giorgio waited patiently as his grandfather spoke with one of the nuns at the front desk. Eventually, she led the two of them back toward the cafeteria where they would deliver their food donations. Once there, Pier Giorgio stood holding his grandfather's hand as he spoke to yet another nun, but the adult conversation bored his juvenile attention span.

He turned to the crowded cafeteria in the adjacent room. Amidst the sea of toddlers hopping about from table to table, he peered into the far corner of the room where the ceiling lights gave way to darkness. There, he noticed a boy sitting alone. Pier Giorgio watched the boy for over a minute, examining his somber face.

In that passing minute, something ached inside Pier Giorgio's heart, something he couldn't explain. The aching he felt, in a peculiar sort of way, also felt soothing. It was a feeling of both pain, but also tenderness, upon seeing this lonesome boy. His solitude engulfed Pier Giorgio, it overwhelmed him. But it wasn't pity, it was love, not the way he loved his family, but love all the same.

The other children, sitting together and enjoying one another's company, did not draw Pier Giorgio's attention the way the lonely boy did, for their happiness blended them into the scenery of the moment, as if they were simply trees in the midst of a forest. But the boy, the one sitting beyond the reach of the ceiling lights, was a like a wandering fawn lost in that forest.

All this occurred to Pier Giorgio, even if only subconsciously, and so he released his hand from his grandfather's.

"Don't go far," Grandfather Ametis said, returning to his conversation with the nun a moment later.

Pier Giorgio navigated his way across the room, sitting down at the table of the secluded boy and speaking plainly.

"Hi, I'm Pier Giorgio."

The boy stared back at him without reply. He was a few years younger than Pier Giorgio, perhaps four years of age.

"And your name?"

"Vincent."

"Why do you sit alone, Vincent?"

"The Sisters said I had to."

"Why?"

"Because of my sickness."

The toddler held up his hands; for the first time Pier

Giorgio noticed a strain of rashes and warts assailing the little boy's skin. Layers of scratch marks ripped across the infected areas like canyons in the earth, stretching to his arms and up towards his face, barely visible above the neckline of his worn and ratty shirt.

Suddenly, Pier Giorgio felt a hand on his shoulder.

"Young man, you shouldn't be sitting here." He turned; above him stood one of the nuns. "You could catch this poor boy's malady."

"I'd like to stay. My grandfather is over there speaking with one of the Sisters. He'll come to get me soon."

She hesitated, opened her mouth, but said nothing and turned and walked away. Pier Giorgio swiveled around in the stool again. He noticed Vincent struggling to lift his spoon from the bowl of soup to his mouth, perhaps from his clumsy and youthful coordination, or perhaps from the difficulties his skin lesions caused him; Pier Giorgio wasn't sure. He took the spoon in his own hand and said, "Here, let me help you, Vincent. We'll both have some soup together. One for me, one for you."

He scooped up a bite of soup and held it to Vincent's mouth. After Vincent had slurped up a bite, Pier Giorgio dipped it again into the steaming soup and took a bite for himself.

"My, this is good!"

Vincent smiled and his face shined like the sun had found him for the first time. Together, the two boys finished the bowl of soup.

4
The Stranger at the Door

The sun hung over Turin amidst a naked, blue sky for most of the day, but the heat had begun to release and settle in the early dusk hours. Pier Giorgio sat alone at his family's dinner table, his legs kicking earnestly. The smell of his mother's gnocchi slowly drifted out of the kitchen and teased his sense of hunger.

Suddenly, there came a knock at the door.

"Alfredo," his mother called out, "will you see who that is?"

Pier Giorgio heard his father grunt from the other room where he sat reading the newspaper. Alfredo Frassati rose from his favorite chair and moved down the hallway toward the front door. Pier Giorgio heard the low rumble of his father's voice and a tense exchange with the guest. His curiosity sprung him toward the front of their house.

"No, we have nothing to give," Alfredo insisted. "Off with you!"

Pier Giorgio peeked around his father's waist and took in the man standing at their front door. He was dressed in rags, wearing a shirt sewn together from dozens of patches. He had dirty hands with grime beneath his fingernails, and his hair was tangled and clumped, as if a bird's nest sat upon his head.

The man pleaded again. "Please, Signor, anything you can spare for a simple beggar..."

"If I must tell you again I'll call the authorities," Alfredo warned as he slammed the door in the man's face. Pier Giorgio reached for the door but his father grabbed his wrist and dragged him down the hallway. Alfredo's hands were moist and sticky from the grease slicking back his hair. "Stay away from the door, Georgie," he commanded. "We have no business with that man."

"But, Papa-"

"I have spoken!"

Adelaide Frassati moved into the hallway, wiping her hands on her apron. "What is all this commotion?"

"Mama," Pier Giorgio pleaded, "there was a poor, hungry man looking for food and Papa has chased him away."

"I'm sure he had his reasons," she said, pulling back strands of her dark hair which had fallen from the pinned-up bun atop her head.

"Oh, Adelaide, if only you could have seen this man, or only smelled him; he reeked of the liquor all those beggars live for."

"But . . ."

"But what, Georgie?" his mother asked.

"Well, maybe it was Jesus who passed by and we've sent him away."

His parents' eyes met before narrowing back on him.

"Georgie," his father said placing his hand on his shoulder, "you have much to learn about the world. Don't try to understand adult matters like this; go and sit there at the table and wait for dinner. I have much work to do this evening."

The young boy moped back to his place at the table as his parents returned to their work. Pier Giorgio heard the clinging of pots echoing from the kitchen and the rustle of his father's newspaper from the den. But the sounds of the house faded into silence as his thoughts returned to the man outside.

The hot weather of summer had probably drained his energy. Pier Giorgio wondered if he could leave the house after everyone had gone to bed and bring this stranger some water and food, if only he could find him. He wondered what else he could do, if perhaps he could sneak the man into their house so he would have a safe roof over his head. Pier Giorgio wondered if his father could get him a job at *La Stampa,* the noted liberal newspaper owned by Signor Frassati. The paper was growing rapidly and perhaps Papa could use some help so that he did not have to work so much himself. Father Cojazzi and the nuns down at the Cathedral were always looking to help people; it was possible that Pier Giorgio could at least send the stranger there. If he went there . . .

"Pier Giorgio!"

His father's voice broke his daze. His family surrounded him, each at the table with hot plates of gnocchi and rising steam before them. His little sister covered her mouth and giggled.

"Hush, Luciana," their mother said. "Georgie, what were you thinking about? Did you not see us here? We've been here for nearly a minute."

"No, I'm sorry."

Everyone at the table picked up their forks and began to cut into their food.

"Are we not going to bless our meal?" the young boy asked.

His father rolled his eyes. The table remained silent, until Pier Giorgio broke into prayer of thanksgiving. When he'd finished, the eating commenced.

"I know what he was thinking about," Alfredo mused, "he was thinking about that bag of dirt that came to our door."

"No need to call him that," his wife corrected.

"But that's what he was."

"Even so."

"So what of it, Dodo, were you thinking of him?"

"Yes, Papa."

"Yes, of course you were. You were wishing you could have helped him like you did some months ago when you gave those beggars with the little child your shoes. Ah . . . yes, you think I didn't know about that? I see the look in your eye; you are a guilty boy, guilty of giving away expensive dress shoes to complete strangers. Forget all this at once, Pier Giorgio. I told you not to concern yourself with that man. I assure you, it was not your Jesus asking for food."

"But shouldn't we act as if it was?"

No one responded. They all continued to eat as Pier Giorgio pushed his food around the plate. This routine, this battle of wills between Pier Giorgio and his parents, was a common one around the Frassati dinner table. Pier Giorgio's parents possessed a tepid faith, if even a faith at all, and wondered how their son could be so different from them. They couldn't fathom the source of his ardent faith. Pier Giorgio, meanwhile, had never known how to be any other way than how he was.

"I tell you what," Adelaide said, "if you're not going to eat this dinner I slaved over, then I'll send one of the servants out into the neighborhood tomorrow to see if this man can be found. Save your own food to give to him. And anyway, you must suddenly hate my gnocchi which you usually devour."

"You'd do this, Mama?"

"No, Georgie, I was only saying that. How difficult you are!"

Alfredo and Luciana laughed.

"But if I eat my dinner and you send someone to find him, we could give him some other food?"

"Fine," she returned with a heavy breath, "just eat your dinner."

The next day Pier Giorgio sat at his desk trying to concentrate on his studies, but his wandering mind precluded much work from getting done. He fiddled with his pencil, flicking it around is desk, then stopped for a moment to watch a bird building a nest in the tree outside his window.

Just then, his parents burst into the room. He quickly returned to the open book on his desk, as if he'd been working the whole time.

"Well," his mother said, "I hope you're happy."

He turned around in his seat. "What?"

"Your friend from yesterday is nothing but a drunk," Alfredo said sternly, "and now we have proof."

Pier Giorgio didn't understand.

His mother clarified. "We sent Valentina out into the streets with a loaf of bread to find your hungry man, your friend of Jesus," she added mockingly. "He was passed out in a gutter with a bottle leaning up against his leg."

"Do you see now, Pier Giorgio?" his father asked. "Do you see why you should listen to us? What nonsense this was."

"Yes, Papa, but did she leave him the bread?"

"You're impossible," his mother said throwing up her hands. "A mad one, you are. Of course she didn't. This man did not deserve our help."

"The bad things he's done don't make him any less hungry, Mama. Besides, what if it really was Jesus who sent us that poor man?"

His father walked toward the door. "I haven't time to deal with this foolishness, Adelaide. Put a stop to it."

His mother scowled and left the room without another word. Pier Giorgio sat alone before the open book, but did not read a word. An unsettling feeling came over him, one that he vowed to avoid in the future. He hated the thought of this man lying hungry in the street. Pier Giorgio knew it was not normal for a boy his age to care about such matters, but he cared all the same.

5

The Providence
of Failure

Pier Giorgio never much minded sharing his favorite tree with Luciana. Unlike most twelve year-old boys he actually welcomed the company of his younger sister. She was only seventeen months his junior, and their proximity in age meant they spent much of their days together. On this summer day, he hoped Luciana could brighten his mood as they sat perched together at the top of a sequoia. It grew from the center of the family's garden bordering their antique villa in Pollone.

"I'm sad the summer is ending," Pier Giorgio lamented. "I don't want to leave Pollone."

"I don't either, Dodo, but every summer must end eventually. Why don't you just return to your songs you were spoiling the countryside with this morning," she added with a chuckle. "That should cheer you up."

"My singing is better than the bird's."

"You cannot carry a tune," she argued back.

"That's only *your* opinion. Parsifal has never complained."

Luciana laughed again. "Yes, horses are loyal like that, even grumpy ones."

He smiled and gazed out at the countryside toward the Mucrone River which snaked about the hills, cutting up the terrain as it flowed steadily toward the south. In the other direction narrow and winding roads divided the surrounding villas with their high, stone walls framing each property. He would miss what this quiet town did to the revival of his spirit. But he also knew there were other reasons the end of this particular summer brought him apprehension. As usual, his sister could read him like a book.

"You mustn't be nervous about changing schools, Georgie. I've heard the Istituto Sociale is a great place. You'll love it."

"I *am* excited to spend time with the Jesuits," he admitted. "But I don't like the thought of being at a different school from you." Luciana nodded, but it appeared she had not yet considered this yet. Pier Giorgio continued, "I suppose I'm just embarrassed I have to change schools."

"You tried your best."

"But mother and father were so upset. They're sending me to the Jesuits because they say I need more discipline with my studies."

"I'm sure you weren't the only one who failed Latin."

"I believe Giuseppe did," he confirmed.

"Well, there you go."

"But this makes me feel no better. What if I don't make good grades at this school either?"

Luciana reached down through the limbs and branches

and patted his back. "I know you will, Dodo. And they'll teach you more about Jesus. That must excite you."

"That's true. Then perhaps I can teach mother and father more about him."

"You know this will not interest them, not unless Jesus purchases one of mother's paintings and can teach father how to increase subscriptions to *La Stampa*."

She chuckled at her own joke but Pier Giorgio did not. His father was never one for going to church, and Pier Giorgio had even heard him question God's existence. His mother, while a woman who did attend Mass with them, rarely, if ever, bothered to receive Communion. She was of the belief that receiving the host only at Christmas and Easter was sufficient. He recalled years ago, when he and Luciana had received their First Holy Communion at the Chapel of the Sister Helpers of the Souls in Purgatory, how she had not possessed the same wonder and excitement he might have hoped for over such an event.

Pier Giorgio looked toward the edge of the garden where his mother sat between rows of rhododendrons, painting the landscape brushed before her. He whispered a prayer that her heart and that of his father's would be opened to the Faith.

The next week the Frassati family returned to Turin, leaving their beloved summer villa in Pollone, and on a hot morning in September Pier Giorgio found himself walking through the front gates of his new school. He was tall for his age, with broad shoulders that demanded attention. The other boys stared at his new face as he found his way toward the main office to check in.

Behind a brown and neatly organized desk sat an older woman with pinned up gray hair and wearing a flower-covered dress. Her rigid face, void of any semblance of a smile, rose from the paperwork she was surveying and suspiciously eyed the young boy standing before her.

"Yes? What do you need, young man?"

"My name is Pier Giorgio Frassati. I'm here for my first day."

"Ah, yes, that's right, the son of Alfredo Frassati. I read *La Stampa*. I find it boring at times but I'll still read it when I have a moment to myself, which is almost never."

Pier Giorgio wasn't sure she was finished. He remained stoic.

"So you want your class schedule, then?"

He nodded, prompting her to rise from her desk and dig through a nearby file cabinet. Just then a man dressed all in black, save for his white collar, emerged from the office behind the receptionist. He was in mid-sentence as he entered past the doorway, looking down at a file of papers.

"Signora Paolo, where is the orientation meeting scheduled for the new parents? It is tonight, no?"

"Yes, Father, tonight. I've reminded you three times now. It's in the Student Commons building. We have one of our new students with us right now. This is Pier Giorgio Frassati."

The priest looked up from his paperwork and smiled.

"Wonderful! Hello, Pier Giorgio, my name is Father Pietro Lombardi." He came forward and shook the young boy's hand.

"It's nice to see you," Pier Giorgio offered.

"And you. Do you know if your parents will be attending the coffee tonight for new parents?"

"I believe my mother will, but not my father."

"Ah, yes, he remains busy with his deadlines, and did I hear he has been made a Senator now as well?" Pier Giorgio nodded. His father had won the prestigious position in the 1913 elections, held just months earlier. "My, you must be proud to have such a distinguished father."

"Yes, my Papa is an amazing man."

The receptionist found what she was looking for and handed Pier Giorgio a sheet of paper.

"Your class schedule," she instructed.

Pier Giorgio glanced down at it and then back at the adults. A haze clouded his expression as he waited for someone to tell him where his first class was.

"I'll walk you there," Father Lombardi offered.

The two of them left the main office and turned down a crowded hallway full of young boys. Fr. Lombardi gave Pier Giorgio a brief tour of the school, but soon the first bell had rung.

"You study hard, Pier Giorgio, and I will see you at Mass."

"At Mass?"

"Yes, of course."

"But it's not Sunday."

"We offer daily Mass here."

"And I may receive the Eucharist?" he asked.

"Of course, if you wish. However, your parents must approve because of your age."

"I'll ask my mother as soon as I see her!"

The priest laughed. "Okay, young man, go take your seat."

Pier Giorgio walked into the room so casually and with such confidence that no other student noticed his unfamiliar face. In the back, beside a row of windows, he found a seat with his name taped to it. He sat down and waited for class to begin.

"Why are you smiling?" he suddenly heard from the boy next to him.

Pier Giorgio turned to meet him. "Smiling?"

"Yes, you're smiling."

"Am I?"

"Yes, as if you are on drugs."

Pier Giorgio laughed. "No, I'm just thrilled by the news that we will be attending Mass daily here, and not just on Sundays."

"Of course we do. It's boring."

"Oh no, it's a joy! We may receive our Lord during the Holy Mass." The boy shrugged. "You must sit next to me at Mass today; I'll show you how amazing the experience is. I'm new here—my name is Pier Giorgio."

The boy received Pier Giorgio's hand. "I'm Anthony. Okay, yes, I'll sit with you at Mass."

"Wonderful!"

A moment later the teacher began his lecture and the boys quieted down. In the midst of taking notes, Pier Giorgio glanced out the window beside him. A horde of trees gathered in front of his view with their branches pushed flush against the window pane. But through a gap in the limbs and leaves he noticed a gold cross rising against the blue sky, resting atop the school's church on the other side of campus. Pier Giorgio smiled and thought to himself how lucky he was to have failed Latin.

6

Mountain Prayers

At dawn, only a few weeks after starting at the Jesuit school, Pier Giorgio set out with his mother toward the neighboring mountains of Turin. The first rays of sun were busy gracing the glistening whitecaps, pushing back the receding shadows of another night passed and gone.

With him he carried his knapsack full of supplies, including those his mother would require to paint the beloved valley which cupped the skyline of their city. Today Pier Giorgio would not climb as high as his usual excursions into the mountains, for his mother only required a view from the elevated plateaus that served as a front porch to the Alps. Still, he brought along food and water for the day-long trip, his ice pick, extra blankets, his spiked boots, and all that his mother would require to capture the city which sat blushed against the scarlet glory of the morning horizon.

They hiked up at a steady but casual pace so his mother could keep up. The air turned crisp and thin and moved quickly through their lungs. When Adelaide had found a spot she fancied, Pier Giorgio unloaded his knapsack, standing up her easel before a large boulder she could sit on and spreading her brushes and paints out on a blanket.

"This is perfect, dear Georgie," his mother said. "I'll be fine here for at least an hour or two. You may go exploring; I know that's what you want to do. But don't go far."

Pier Giorgio leaned down and kissed her on the cheek. "Paint me a masterpiece, Mama."

He set off further into the mountain trees and disappeared from the world of men. It was here that Pier Giorgio found solace from the daily stresses of his life—his studies, his parents' indifference to God, the shame he felt for any sins he had committed, no matter how trivial they were. He viewed the mountains as a link between heaven and earth, and often pretended he could climb all the way to St. Peter's gate if only he could impede the darkness of the night. A step was not taken without a prayer to accompany it, a prayer for those he loved and ones for his own sanctity, as well as a request for good weather so his mother could complete her painting.

He found a small cave some three hundred yards above where he had left his mother and rested at the opening where he sat praying to the Virgin Mother. A familiar comfort came over him as his soul fell into her arms. His prayers often returned to her, as if by instinct, like the waves perpetually returning to the shore. Even as a young adolescent he strove each day to nurture his relationship with the mother of Christ, so that through her, he might find perfect devotion to Christ himself. As Christ was born into the world through her, he hoped the Savior might be born into his soul in the same manner. He found consolation in his prayers to Mary, especially when he meditated on the relationship he had with his own mother and the love he felt for her.

Later, he explored the mountainside, collecting rocks, minerals, and pebbles that caught his eye, a habit his mother was not fond of. The windowsill in his bedroom was covered in such things and she often raided his room to clean them up.

In time, he found his way back down the mountain where his mother sat painting on the boulder. He called out to her from a distance.

"Even from here I see the beauty in your brushstrokes, Mama!"

She turned and smiled. When he reached her he dug into his bag and prepared their picnic lunch.

"And what did you find up there, Georgie?" she asked, biting into an apple.

"I find something new every time I journey into these high lands. Today I found a cave."

"I hope you didn't go in it! Who knows what beasts could've been waiting inside?"

He laughed as he sat down on the ground below her. "No, I didn't go inside. I sat at the entrance and enjoyed the view."

Adelaide took a sip of water and wiped her mouth with a napkin. "I know that's not all you did. Those pockets of yours seem fuller than when you left."

"I have no idea what you're talking about," he answered playfully.

"Georgie, I had that talk with Father Lombardi."

His jovial expression fell toward the ground. He hoped

his prayers earlier in the day had been answered.

"He is a good man, Mama."

"I never said he wasn't. I just needed to talk with him about your desire to receive the Eucharist each day."

"Yes, I need your permission as a minor."

"I'm fully aware. You've asked me a dozen times in the last week alone."

"And?" he asked wishfully.

She looked out toward the city of Turin before answering. "I cannot figure you out, Pier Giorgio. Father Lombardi tells me they have to drag the other boys into the pews, but they must drag you *out* of them."

He hung his head and fidgeted with his fingers.

"He said you want to join every club they have—the Eucharistic Crusade, the Apostolate of Prayer, The Marian Sodality—and all the others. I can't even recall them all. All this focus on the Catholic faith is not normal for our family."

"Grandmother Ametis has always been very pious, Mama."

"Yes, but oh, how she doesn't live in this world. I wonder if she could even tell you who our Prime Minster is." Pier Giorgio didn't respond. "Are you not concerned that if you are to receive the Eucharist each and every day it will become a practice which lacks meaning?"

"This miracle could never lack meaning."

Adelaide stared at her son; he stared back.

"I don't wish to keep you from your Jesus," she finally said. "I'm merely concerned about you becoming too focused on religious matters. Your father and I don't want a narrow-minded Catholic as a son. We are not raising a priest, Giorgio. You will have to focus on your studies and follow the world of politics more if you're to take over *La Stampa* for your father one day."

"What if that's not what I want to do?"

"Hush, boy! It will be an honor to hold the prestige your father does."

"What about Luciana? She would be more suited to follow in Papa's footsteps."

"Nonsense. She's a woman. Don't be absurd."

The two of them ate in silence as the high winds of the hills blew across their faces. Adelaide sighed.

"Despite all I've said, I did give Father Lombardi my permission to allow you to receive Communion each day."

"Oh, Mama, you did?"

"But you must not neglect your studies by spending all your time in those pews."

"Of course not. Mama, thank you. Thank you from the bottom of my heart!" He rose and threw his arms around her neck, then turned toward the city of Turin and shouted, "Now hear this, citizens of *Italia*! I have the best mother in all these great lands!"

Adelaide laughed and blushed. "Sit down, you silly boy."

Over the next year, Pier Giorgio began to revolve each day of his life around his reception of the Eucharist. It became as common as brushing his teeth. For him, a day without receiving Christ was a day lost in the shadows of despair. Thus, a happy period of his life commenced, one in which the joys outweighed the sorrows and he grew closer to leaving his boyhood behind.

But on June 28, 1914, just after his thirteenth birthday, the assassination of Archduke Francis Ferdinand of Austria and his wife Sofia changed everything. Soon, all of Europe was engulfed in the flames of war.

7

Fists after Mass

Pier Giorgio sat on the curb outside of school reading the day's *La Stampa* as his breath cut through the frigid, winter air. A light snow caked the ground and crunched beneath him each time he shuffled his feet. He normally did not bother to read much of his father's paper but had read every word of every issue in the last months as the debate raged on concerning his country's involvement in the conflict ripping Europe apart.

"Sorry for making you wait," he heard from behind him. The shadow cast by his friend, Camillo Banzatti, moved across his body. Pier Giorgio turned and smiled.

"It's no problem. Did you speak with your teacher?"

"Yes, all is well. Shall we walk home?"

Pier Giorgio rose to his feet and threw his backpack over his shoulder as the two moved down the street. He kept reading the paper as he walked but struggled to hold it with his mittens on.

"I feel our fathers are facing backlash over the stance their paper has taken against the war," he said.

Camillo glanced at the paper but not long enough to read the article Pier Giorgio was reading. He shrugged. "I'm too young to understand the complications of war."

"You mustn't say this, Camillo. Our fathers are right to stand with Prime Minister Giolitti. We must support them."

"I've heard that Gabriele D'Annunzio is in favor of us joining the war. He and others feel victory will come swiftly if only we would do our part."

"I am just as big a fan of D'Annunzio's literary work as anyone, but I fail to understand why we should listen to a poet in matters of war."

"He is very influential," Camillo offered. "My father thinks he's having an effect on the people."

"Perhaps."

They turned down a narrow, side road away from the passing of cars and buses. This less-traveled road was still covered in a blanket of snow. They had not gone ten feet when they heard a shout from behind them.

"Mercenaries!"

The two boys turned around. Mario Attilio Levi, their classmate from school, stood there.

"Yes, you heard me. Mercenaries. That's what you are, traitors and mercenaries."

Mario took a few steps closer to them, his fists clenched. Pier Giorgio knew what this was about. He had felt the stares and heard the whispers at school each time he and Camillo walked by.

"We don't want any trouble, Mario," Pier Giorgio reasoned.

"Your fathers are traitors, and so are you. They poison people with their paper and try to convince them to not stand up for our country."

"Take it back!" Camillo yelled.

"They're not traitors," Pier Giorgio broke in. "They simply don't support the actions of sending our young men into war. This has nothing to do with not loving *Italia*."

"Traitors!" he yelled again. "That's just an excuse traitors use."

Camillo threw down his backpack and lunged forward, taking his classmate to the snowy asphalt in less than a second. Pier Giorgio jumped back, disbelieving what was taking place before him. He ripped off his mittens and headed toward the two boys rolling in the snow, but withheld for a moment. He watched as Mario snuck in a right hook that connected with Camillo's nose, drawing immediate blood. But Camillo did not waver for an instant and returned a punch that landed on Mario's right ear. They tried to put each other in headlocks but unsuccessfully. Again, Pier Giorgio moved toward the fight, but then took a step back.

A moment later a passing woman took note of what was happening.

"Hey, what are you boys doing? Stop that! Stop that at once!" She turned to the other side of the road and saw a police officer. "Officer! Officer! Over here!"

Pier Giorgio swooped in and pulled Camillo away from Mario. They scooped up their bags and ran down the alley, turning back once to see Mario running in the other direction away from the police officer.

They ran all the way to Camillo's house and barged through the front door. They were met by Signora Banzatti who became hysterical at the sight of blood dripping from her son's nose like water from a faucet.

"What happened?" she asked, running for ice and a towel.

Camillo relayed the story, but halfway through the tale his father walked in the house and he was forced to start over. Pier Giorgio could tell Signor Banzatti felt guilty that his political views from *La Stampa* had led to his son's injuries.

Not much later, Signor Banzatti drove Pier Giorgio home, not wanting him to face any more trouble in walking the rest of the way. He escorted him to the house and told the story to Pier Giorgio's parents. Alfredo Frassati kept eyeing his son as he listened to the dramatic tale, twice grabbing Pier Giorgio's face to inspect it.

"I'll see you tomorrow at work, Alfredo," Signor Banzatti said as he left the house. "We will discuss what to do about this then."

The moment he was gone Pier Giorgio's parents cornered him. Luciana watched from the entry to the kitchen.

"Why do you not have any bruises and scars like Camillo?" his father asked.

Pier Giorgio hesitated. "I was not the one who fought, Papa."

He huffed and his mother rolled her eyes. "So you left it up to Camillo to defend our family's honor, then? I suppose I'm glad Camillo is not a coward and has the courage to stand up for us."

"Why did you not help Camillo?" his mother asked.

Pier Giorgio hung his head and mumbled inaudibly.

"What did you say?" Alfredo asked of his son.

"I said it wouldn't have been fair."

"What do you mean?"

"It was only the three of us in the snowy alley. If I had joined in, it would have been two against one."

His mother laughed, but not in good humor. "Only you would care about that, Giorgio. Was he not the one who attacked you two? You should have let him have it."

"Tomorrow it will be my turn," he said, but his father had left the room shaking his head and his mother didn't seem to hear him as she began to prepare dinner.

That night Pier Giorgio slept little, tossing in his sheets as if bugs lay beside him. He rose early the next day before the rest of the family and left the house, walking several blocks to the Cathedral in the frozen morning so he could attend Mass and received the Eucharist.

After Mass, he scurried out of the church and ran all the way to school as a light snow began to fall. The hallways were packed but he navigated his way quickly through the bodies like a fish swimming through the sea and arrived at where he knew Mario Attilio Levi would be standing waiting to enter his first class of the day. His back was to Pier Giorgio but the latter could hear him relaying the story of the fight to a group of boys, embellishing his successful triumph over Camillo.

"Mario," he said tapping the boy on the shoulder. Mario turned around. "Today it is my turn."

Pier Giorgio drew back his fist and threw it at Mario's nose. A roar erupted from the students around them as Mario fell to the ground. Pier Giorgio turned and walked directly toward the Principal's office with a smile stuck square on his face.

8

Sympathy for Soldiers

Pier Giorgio was devastated when on May 24, 1915 Italy declared war on Austria. Over the next months dozens of young men were sent off to the front lines, many of them returning in body bags just weeks later. One of the Frassati family servants, Natalina, lost her brother and cried in Pier Giorgio's arms upon finding out.

"I'd give my own life to end this dreadful war," he told her, clutching her sobbing body. "But do not weep, for your brother is with Christ and his most Holy Mother."

He withdrew into periods of great silence and despair when he thought about the war—its soldiers, widows, and even the fallen of the "enemy." Despite how hard it was, he read about the battles as much as possible, feeling that he could only know how and what to pray for if he was properly informed.

Pier Giorgio shuddered at reading about the newest weapon being used in warfare, that of poisonous gas. Thousands of soldiers were killed when gaseous clouds descended down from the sky, drowning their lungs in fire. If any survived, their skin was scarred for life.

Although the battles never made their way to the Frassati doorstep, a cloud of discomfort, tension and sadness hung over all of Turin. Friends were lost in political arguments due to Alfredo's public position of neutrality, so much so that Pier Giorgio's boyish tiff with Mario Attilio Levi was all but forgotten.

Pier Giorgio made it his mission to do anything he could for the wounded returning from battle. He took up every lira he could find and hand-delivered it to the soldiers lying in crowded hospital beds, then sat down and prayed with them. He went and spoke at their clubs, offering encouraging words and ideas for how to transition back into everyday life. All were amazed by the wisdom which extended beyond his teenage years.

In the midst of his work with the returning soldiers, he met a young man named Gianni Brunelli. Gianni was a member of the Alpine Brigade, which was an integral division of the Italian Army. As soon as Pier Giorgio heard of Gianni's tales in the mountains the two became close friends. They exchanged stories about their adventures in the snowy mountains and compared trails and locations they had visited.

"One day soon we must climb together," Pier Giorgio offered as the two of them sat at a café.

"Absolutely," Gianni replied. "I'd welcome an excursion into the mountains for fun. Most of my recent trips were for missions."

Pier Giorgio nodded sympathetically. "I feel a deep sadness for what you and your brothers have seen in battle. I suppose I'd have been there with you had I been a few years older. I'm sorry I couldn't fight alongside you, despite my opposition to this war."

"You do your part, Pier Giorgio. The men of my company appreciate all you've done for us."

"I'd love to meet more of them. Did you invite them to Mass as I suggested?"

Gianni shook his head. "They'll never come with me. They're bitter towards a God who allows what they've seen in battle. None of them have been to Mass since returning home."

"But have you at least asked them and suggested they come?"

"No, but I'm confident of their refusal."

"We can never assume someone wants to avoid Christ. Let them tell us with their own mouths. We may fail, but then we can look God in the eye and tell Him we tried. Tell them, only if they feed on the Bread of Angels will they be able to combat the inner demons that have tormented them since their return from battle. Besides, it is man who performs the evil deeds of war, not God. Will you at least ask them if they will join us this Sunday? What will it hurt to ask? Please, Gianni, you must ask. They don't realize how important the Mass can be for their renewal of spirit."

Gianni considered his words. "Okay. You've done much for me, so I will do this for you. But don't expect anyone to accompany me."

Pier Giorgio smiled. "Even if it's only you, I'll be thrilled to receive the Eucharist alongside you."

Two days passed and Sunday arrived. Pier Giorgio awoke on the floor, a rosary in his hand. He had done it again, praying until sleep overtook him. If his mother had seen him she would have been upset. "I don't even know why we got you a bed," she once said. He bathed himself and dressed in his nicest clothes. Today, he would be the only one from his family attending Mass, but as he rode his bike to the Cathedral in Turin he thought only of Gianni and his fellow soldiers.

Although to Pier Giorgio most of them were faceless men, he had pictured them with each passing bead of his rosary the previous night. Each man, each stranger, so wounded by the horrors of war, was represented by a bead. They became the beneficiary of one Hail Mary as they passed between Pier Giorgio's fingers and moved within him to reside in his soul, the sanctuary that inhabited all those he prayed for. To his new friend Gianni, he devoted a whole decade.

He waited out front for Gianni just as he had done the previous two Sundays, nodding and smiling at those walking past the massive doors and into the narthex of the Cathedral. He glanced at his watch—four minutes until Mass began. He poked his head into the Church to see if he could see his friend. Perhaps Gianni had forgotten that they would meet out front. But he did not see him.

Pier Giorgio scurried back outside to check one last time. He turned and looked down the street. There in the distance he saw a soldier in uniform walking briskly down the street, with nearly two dozen of his fellow soldiers walking behind him, also in uniform. Many of them limped and others had their arms in slings. One was being led by the hand of a friend, his eyes masked in bandages, and another's skin had turned so red from scars it looked as though his entire face had been torn off, no doubt from the poisonous gas.

"Are we late?" Gianni asked as he approached.

"No, my friend, you're right on time, and all are welcome. So many you have brought with you!"

"I don't know what it was, Georgie. Every man I asked said yes. It was as if they knew what I was coming to ask them before I even spoke. Strange, no?"

Pier Giorgio smiled. "No, Gianni, not strange at all."

He led them into the Cathedral and filled up the last three rows with the souls of wounded soldiers.

9

Remembering the Forgotten

Pier Giorgio laughed as Camillo ran toward the bushes and threw up his dinner. The sound of his friend getting sick would not normally bring him such delight, but he couldn't help himself.

"Ah, Camillo, you're not such a big shot now, are you? What were you saying about looking so grown up smoking that cigar?"

Camillo collected himself and wiped at his mouth. "How can you smoke these so casually?" he asked. "One puff has churned up my stomach."

"What do you expect?" Pier Giorgio said with a chuckle. "My mother smokes cigars. She smoked them as she breast fed me."

Camillo put out his cigar on the ground and hurled it across the patio at Pier Giorgio. The latter dodged it and hurled a small pebble back at Camillo. Pier Giorgio enjoyed such casual moments with friends, moments that he knew would begin to dwindle with adulthood and all its responsibilities quickly approaching.

"I hope I haven't ruined our Sunday evening with my vomiting," Camillo said, returning to his seat alongside Pier

Giorgio on the Frassati back patio. He grabbed a glass of water resting on the table and swished a small sip in his mouth to wash out the stale taste before spitting it back out.

"Nonsense. This has been a blessed day. I awoke and visited Christ in the Blessed Sacrament, I enjoyed a bike ride below glorious sunshine, I ate my mother's wonderful cooking for dinner, and now I'm able to watch you throw up that very dinner as I enjoy this Tuscan cigar. What else could a boy ask for?"

"There's always more to ask for. Perhaps we should walk down to a café and see what girls are there," Camillo suggested.

"Oh, Camillo, how do you always have the same thing on your mind?"

"I could ask you the same thing, always thinking of your Jesus."

"Yes, but my Jesus helps to keep me out of Purgatory, while your girls will send you straight there if you are not careful."

Camillo laughed and playfully poked at his friend's shoulder. "Come on, Georgie, let's see what trouble we can get into down the road."

Pier Giorgio took a long drag on his cigar, blowing out the smoke slow and steady as Camillo waited for an answer with baited breath.

"I'm sorry, Camillo, I cannot journey into town."

"What? Why not?"

"I must attend early Mass tomorrow before school. I should get to bed soon."

"Oh, friend, what need do you have for Mass tomorrow?

It's not Sunday. I need your good looks to help attract the girls down at the café. You know how they love those dark eyes and long lashes of Pier Giorgio Frassati, the one and only Senator's son!"

Pier Giorgio smiled. "You need no one's help with the girls, and certainly not mine. But I'm sorry, it's a very important day and I cannot miss Mass."

"What's tomorrow?" Camillo asked, receding temporarily into his mind to try to place the date.

"I would rather not say," Pier Giorgio responded. "It's just a private matter of prayer that's very important. But perhaps you should just journey home instead of to the café anyway; tomorrow is a school day."

"Yes, I'm aware. I did not realize I was smoking cigars with my mother here on this fine night."

"Are you comparing me to an old woman when you were the one getting sick from a little cigar smoke?"

"Ah! I cannot wait to tell Mama that Pier Giorgio called her an 'old woman.' You will no longer be her favorite!"

The two boys laughed and rose from the patio table. Pier Giorgio escorted Camillo out to the street and waved goodbye before returning to the back patio to enjoy the last of his cigar. Moonlight fell from the sky and illuminated a bird's nest nestled snuggly in a branch above him.

"Oh, little birdies," he said aloud, "what am I to do with my life? I'm nearly finished with high school and I must determine my path. I've begun to wonder if God is calling me to the clergy. I know I'd be happy as a priest, but Mama and Papa would not wish this of my future. They would delight in my taking over *La Stampa* and following in Papa's footsteps; they have all but told me this from their very mouths. What do you think, birdies? Shall I honor their wishes, or follow my heart?"

No response came from the nest above him.

"Birdies? Are you there? Lately, I have felt a strong attraction to the poor of my city. I feel a call to help them in any way I can, and I suppose I can help them just as much as a layman as I could as a priest, perhaps more. Birdies, what do you think? Are you there? Won't you sing to me in the evenings as you sing to me in the mornings? Shall I sing to you instead?"

He closed his eyes and broke into song, his voice breaking and missing every note and pitch of the love ballad he delivered to the sleeping birds above him. A moment later, a window overlooking the patio opened and his mother's head poked out.

"Georgie! Stop with your horrible singing; you will wake the neighbors; cars are probably crashing in the streets!"

"Oh, Mama," he called up to her, "you're breaking your son's heart! Won't you let me sing to you?"

"No, go to bed!"

She slammed the window just before his laughter reached her ears. He put out his cigar and rose from the table.

"Well, goodnight birdies."

The next morning he arose early and used the service staircase reserved for the servants, so as to not wake his family, and left early for Mass. The sun was just peeking over the edge of Turin, its bright rays funneling down the city streets between the homes and buildings.

He attended Mass and received the Blessed Sacrament, then stayed after and prayed before a statue of the Virgin surrounded by the glow of votive candles. At one point his body began to tremble and tears gathered in his eyes. A group of older women praying in the pews behind him wondered if he was alright, but they withheld from checking on him. There seemed to be a presence around him that kept others from approaching.

After Mass, he walked several blocks over to school. His friends hollered and greeted him with warm smiles as he entered the school courtyard, but Camillo did not. He recalled what Pier Giorgio had told him about needing to pray this morning and sensed that his friend needed to be alone, needed to do something before he went on with his day. Pier Giorgio ignored all the other students and walked over toward a row of trashcans where the school custodian stood emptying them.

"Mr. Ernesto?"

The man turned and smiled, wiping his hands on his sleeves before extending one to greet Pier Giorgio. "Good morning, Georgie!"

Pier Giorgio moved past Ernesto's hand and hugged him.

"Pier Giorgio, what is this?"

When Pier Giorgio pulled back, Ernesto saw the red in his eyes.

"What's the matter, dear boy? Are you alright?"

Other students watched from a few yards away, wondering why Pier Giorgio would bother to hug a man no one even talked to.

"Mr. Ernesto, I know this is the anniversary of your son's death. I remembered him at the altar today when I received the Eucharist, and I prayed to the Most Holy Virgin to watch over you during this time of sadness."

"How . . ." he faltered. "How is it that you remember this?"

"We spoke last year on this day, when I noticed how upset you were. You told me of the death of your young son. My heart breaks for your sorrow, Ernesto, but I know your sufferings will bring you glory in heaven."

"Georgie, I . . . I don't know what to say. It seems those in our own family have already forgotten my son, and yet you have begun your day with thoughts of him."

Ernesto began to cry and Pier Giorgio held him again. He held him for several minutes, until the morning bell rung.

10

Bells for Peace

Pier Giorgio awoke at dawn to the peculiar clink of his bedside table's metal handle banging against the wood of the drawer. It rose and fell in rapid succession three times by the pulling of a rope, paused, then three clinks again.

He rubbed his eyes and rose from bed, sliding over toward the window as he followed the rope which dangled out of his room and fell down the side of the house. He poked his head outside and waved down to Signora Gola. She smiled and waved back.

He dressed and quietly made his way outside to meet her. An orange blanket and a lazy mist hung over the Pollone countryside. On the ground, the early-morning autumn dew had turned crisp below his feet as he circled the house to where the family garden grew.

"Good morning!" he exclaimed upon reaching her.

"And good morning to you," she replied. "You're enthusiastic even at this early hour. Most boys your age want only to sleep on their Saturdays."

"Working in the garden with you is far better than sleeping."

"I'm not so sure about that, but you're kind to say

so. Are you sure about the way in which I wake you each morning, though?"

"Of course. It's better that you pull the rope from out here so as to not wake anyone else by coming in the house. You don't want to see Mama this early in the morning. She can be very grumpy if her sleep is prematurely interrupted."

She chuckled. "I believe we're all that way. Thank you again for your help, Georgie. I will be sure to tell my husband if he makes it back that you've helped me keep up his duties while he's away."

"He *will* make it home, Signora, I know he will. My father thinks the war will be over soon, maybe by the end of this month."

"I hope so. He'll be happy to see the garden looking so nice," she said looking out over the greenery framed by a stone wall. "I could not have done all this without your help this summer."

"Say nothing more. Your husband has been a loyal worker for my family for years, and is serving our country bravely. It's the least I can do. But please, let us set out to work. These potatoes are not going to dig themselves up."

The two of them disappeared into the rows of crops and flowers and worked for two hours before anyone else in the house had emerged from their beds. The sun rose slowly into the sky and bronzed Pier Giorgio's olive skin, just as it had done each day throughout the last weeks. He enjoyed the manual labor and looked at it as physical training for his mountain excursions. He was growing into a sturdy young man and it showed even through his clothes.

After their labors were complete, Pier Giorgio plucked a daisy and headed toward the house, waving back to Signora Gola. "I'll see you tomorrow, or perhaps sooner!"

"Yes, I hope so. Is that flower for a young woman who has attracted your interest?"

"Of course not!" he shouted without turning around. "You know Mama is the only woman for me!"

She chuckled as she watched him walk back around the house. Inside, Pier Giorgio found his mother and sister sitting down to breakfast. His father was still asleep upstairs after arriving in the middle of the night from Turin where he had stayed late working.

"Where have you been?" his mother asked.

"Working in the garden with Signora Gola. Here, mother, I have picked you the most pleasant-smelling daisy from our garden."

She took the flower and laid it on the table before walking into the kitchen. "You don't need to get in her way. Stay out of there while she's working."

Pier Giorgio glanced down at the daisy, then to Luciana. His sister smiled and reached across the table for the flower, holding it beneath her nose.

"My, this does smell wonderful. What a pleasant smell so early in the morning. May I have it, Georgie?"

He smiled. "Yes, please."

Adelaide returned from the kitchen with a plate full of eggs and fruit. "Did you hear me? Stay out of the garden and let her do her work."

"I was only trying to help while Signor Gola is off at war."

"But I know you; you will distract her with your singing and your talking, whether you mean to or not."

The three of them sat down to eat but spoke little as Adelaide read the paper. Her children could tell she didn't want to be distracted by conversation. Minutes later, the sound of Alfredo's footsteps creaking upstairs signaled his impending arrival to their family breakfast. Luciana ran and hugged him before he could finish descending the stairs.

"We've missed you, Papa!" she said, throwing her arms around him.

"And I you," he replied, laughing. "But let me eat something before you knock me down. I'm weak with hunger."

Pier Giorgio rose with a smile and hugged his father. It had been two weeks since Alfredo Frassati had seen his children. His long hours at work and their weekend excursions up to Pollone had precluded many family meals.

"I'm glad you could get away from work, Papa."

"Yes, but only for now," Alfredo said, taking his seat at the head of the table. Pier Giorgio and Luciana returned to their seats as well. Adelaide had not risen or looked up from her paper to greet her husband.

"I must return to Turin tomorrow, quite early in the morning," he continued. "With the war nearing an end, we're very busy trying to report on everything."

"You must leave early on a Sunday?" Pier Giorgio asked. "Were we not going to have a picnic by the river?"

"Yes, I must leave at dawn, and don't start with me, son. I don't dictate when the news arises; I must simply report on it."

"Well, I don't want you to leave, but the end of this

dreaded war would be a nice consolation for missing my Papa."

Alfredo smiled. "Now tell me," he said, poking a strawberry with his fork and shoving it into his mouth as the red juice gathered on his moustache, "what about my children have I missed? What have you to report?"

"I've joined the choir society at school," Luciana began. "I was nervous at first to sing in front of others. I had to sing a solo, Papa; oh, you should have seen me. My palms were sweating and-"

"Adelaide," he interrupted, "won't you get me some wine?"

She looked up from her paper for the first time. "This early in the morning? Even for you that's strange."

"I've asked something and expect to get it," he replied frankly, never once meeting her eyes with his. "And what about you, Georgie?" he asked, turning to his son. "We've heard from Luciana. Now, tell me what you've been doing with your time, and what are your plans for the future?"

Pier Giorgio glanced at Luciana but her head was hung.

"Well, I received my high school diploma last month," he began.

"Yes, that's right. How proud I am of you. Have you decided on what gift you would like? My offer still stands, would you like a car? Or the money I would spend to get you a car?"

Pier Giorgio thought for a moment. "I believe I'd like the money, Papa. Both offers are very generous of you, but if you're leaving this decision to me, I'll take the money."

"Very well." He took a large sip of his orange juice.

"Mama will give it to you when we get back to Turin. And what else, Georgie? What of your future plans?"

"I have decided to enroll at the Royal Polytechnic. I want to specialize in mining engineering."

Alfredo nearly choked on his eggs.

"What? What sort of education is that?"

Pier Giorgio collected himself and glanced down to his feet, as if searching for an answer to his father's question below the table.

"It's my dream to work beside miners and help improve their working and living conditions. They've been exploited for years. You know this, Papa; *La Stampa* has written about it."

"Yes, but let someone else do something about it. What good will a mining degree do you in taking over for me at the paper?" Pier Giorgio did not answer. "What of it, then, son?"

"I'm not sure, Papa. But perhaps I can volunteer at *La Stampa* on my days off. Certainly you have some employees who lack an education in the news and print business."

"Yes, some, perhaps a custodian or two."

"Good, then I shall help them with their work."

"Oh, don't be absurd," his mother broke in, handing Alfredo his wine. Alfredo took it and gulped down half the glass.

"How funny it is that my brother, who so loves to climb the mountains with a passion like no other, wants to journey *beneath* them as a profession."

Luciana laughed at her own observation.

"I had not considered it that way," Pier Giorgio

admitted. "But yes, I suppose that's true."

The admission brought him a smile.

"We'll talk about this later," Alfredo said. "I must return to bed." He left his family to their breakfast. Pier Giorgio and Luciana glanced at each other, but neither spoke.

* * * * *

Hours later, Alfredo was jarred from his nap by the sounds of tree branches pushing up against his window. They swayed in the afternoon wind and scratched the glass pane. He rose and approached the window.

Down below, in the pasture of tall grass, Pier Giorgio rested on his knees, his back to the house. Even without seeing his face, Alfredo knew his son's eyes were closed and he was deep in prayer.

Just then, Adelaide walked in with a handful of recently washed and ironed clothes. Alfredo turned. "What're you doing with those? Where's Natalina?"

"She went home early, very sick. You don't think I know how to wash and put away clothes? I don't need a maid to do everything for me."

He said nothing and turned back toward the window.

"What're you looking at?"

"Our pious son."

Curious, she placed the clothes on the bed and walked across the room, joining him at the window. She watched their son for a moment before speaking.

"Where does he get it from?" she asked.

"I haven't a clue."

They both watched, as if waiting for Pier Giorgio to

stop praying, as willing him to stop. He didn't.

"I went to speak with Fr. Roccati last month," Alfredo suddenly said.

"Concerning what?"

"I told him I was troubled by how much time Pier Giorgio spends with that rosary he gave him."

"And what did he say?"

Alfredo looked over to his wife. "He asked would I rather Pier Giorgio be spending that much time with a trashy magazine."

"What an awful thing for a priest to say!"

Alfredo chuckled. "I found it rather witty."

Their gaze fell back outside just when Luciana walked out the side door and approached Pier Giorgio with a picnic basket. Pier Giorgio placed his rosary in his pocket, rose to his feet, and the two of them set out across the pasture.

"That is a strange son we have," Adelaide said, watching her children disappear over a hill. "Sometimes I wonder if he isn't someone else's child."

Alfredo pursed his lips, nodded, and said, "Strange, yes, but he gives me the impression I am meeting someone older than myself. I don't know what I mean by that, but nonetheless, he gives me that impression."

Adelaide looked over to her husband, opened her mouth briefly to reply, but instead turned back toward the bed to put away the clothes.

* * * * *

Pier Giorgio and Luciana strolled down to the river with a picnic basket they had filled with sandwiches, fruit, and juice, the food that was supposed to be for their family picnic the next day.

"I didn't see any dessert in this basket," Luciana said, taking off her shoes and dipping them into the water. "No candy?"

"No," Pier Giorgio responded, sitting down alongside her. "I know about your punishment for talking back to Mama yesterday."

"That doesn't mean *you* cannot have any candy."

"No, but I don't want to have any when you cannot, and besides, why provide such a temptation for you?"

She smiled, squinting as she looked at him with the sunlight over his shoulders.

"You should've taken the car from Papa," she advised, changing the subject.

"Perhaps."

"That's what I would have done. People expect to see us with nice things like a car, being the son of Alfredo Frassati. I like to fulfill their expectations," she added with a smirk. He shrugged as he picked at the blades of grass around him. "Well, why didn't you take the car, then?"

"I'd rather have the money."

"Do you forget that I'm your best friend?"

"What do you mean by that?"

"I know you, Georgie. I know you're up to something. You're not like me, or anyone else for that matter. Money does not interest you. I thought at least a car would."

"It's not that money does not interest me, or a car, it's just," he paused and smiled, "giving away money is easier than giving away a car."

"I knew it! And just who will be the beneficiary of Papa's money?"

"I saw a flyer for the St. Vincent de Paul Society the other day. They serve the poor and I may wish to join. I anticipate the money will help if I do. You will not tell Papa, no?"

"Your secret is safe with me, but how about you donate to the Luciana fund before journeying off to visit the poor of Turin?"

Pier Giorgio chuckled. "You're doing just fine, sister."

They opened their basket and ate together as the autumn winds swirled atop the current of the nearby river. The weather had turned colder in the last week, signaling the impending arrival of winter. Pier Giorgio glanced at his sister when she was not looking, wondering what he would do without her. For him, she was the glimmer of sunlight poking through the gloomy clouds which often hung over the family during his parents' arguments.

After their lunch, they journeyed back up the house. An unfamiliar car was pulling out of their driveway, but it fled from sight before they could make out the driver. Both of them ran inside, shocked to find their parents popping open a bottle of champagne.

"What's going on?" Luciana asked.

Their parents, not seeing their children for a moment, kissed, and each took a swing straight from the bottle.

"Mama, Papa, what's going on?" she asked again.

Alfredo turned to his children. "Come, celebrate with us; we're no longer at war!"

"What?" Pier Giorgio exclaimed.

"Papa has just received a telegram," his mother said. "The war is over!"

Pier Giorgio turned and hugged his sister, lifting her off the ground and swinging her so easily it was as if she was a feather. They ran to hug their parents, and even partook in the celebratory champagne. Then suddenly, Pier Giorgio sprinted out of the room.

"Where are you going, Georgie?" his mother called after him.

"Signora Gola! Someone must tell her!"

Pier Giorgio sprinted out of the house and turned down the narrow road leading to the town of Pollone. He was halfway there when he realized he didn't know where the wife of their gardener lived. The only way in which he could foresee remedying this situation was to turn toward the church. He burst through the front doors and climbed the bell tower. A few feet below the bells, he grabbed the giant chains and began to pull them as fast as he could. The bells rang so loudly his voice could narrowly be heard.

"Attention! Attention! Citizens of Pollone! The war is over! Signora Gola, your husband is coming home to you! Do you hear me? The war is over!"

For five more minutes he rang the bells and screamed at the top of his lungs, until soon he caught the ire of an elderly and frustrated nun who came to scurry him away. Once outside, he found dozens of townspeople slowly wandering into the square to investigate the unexpected commotion in their normally sleepy town. He scanned the crowd until he found her, sprinting straight for Signora Gola and hugging her.

"Did you hear? The war is over! Your husband is coming home!" When he pulled away, he discovered all she could do was weep for joy. "Wait until he sees the work you've done in the garden while he was away; his eyes will grow as wide as the potatoes!"

Laughter broke through her tears, and again the two of them embraced.

11

A Chosen Path

All of Italy celebrated the end of the war in the weeks leading up to Christmas of 1918. Pier Giorgio joined in the festivities, staying out half the night with his friends. He wandered the streets of Turin with a cigar in his hand, singing at the top of his lungs and hugging complete strangers. Bliss ran through his veins at the sight and feel of what peace did to his brethren.

But on a brisk day in late November he decided to follow through on a promise he had made to himself. He arose early and rode his bike to the Cathedral of Turin to attend Mass. Afterwards, he rushed back home and picked as many flowers as he could from the family garden, then journeyed across town to an area he rarely found himself in—a broken, gutter-like row of slums on the opposite side of the city.

He had read about this ghetto in a flyer from the St. Vincent de Paul Society, a religious foundation who served the poor of his city. Their newsletter detailed the ghastly conditions these residents lived among—the crime, the dilapidated housing, the poor sewage system, the dirty water, and the disease that often spread throughout the streets. His curiosity to see these things firsthand had driven him here.

First, however, he journeyed to the local cemetery where the people of this neighborhood were buried. In the paperwork he had read, he noticed a picture of the abandoned graveyard, with its crumbling tombstones overrun by weeds and other brush. Pier Giorgio knew the only thing more ignored than the poor of society were the deceased of the poor.

He got off his bike, resting it against the rickety outer gate of the cemetery, and walked inside to scan the rows of tombstones, reading the names aloud in a soft whisper. He wondered if the fallen could hear him, or if their names had been missing from the lips of the living for so long they no longer recognized it. He began to rip away as much of the weeds as he could and placed the flowers he had picked from the garden at the foot of each grave. When he ran out of flowers, he went back and plucked apart the pedals and ripped off pieces of the stems, placing what he could at every grave so that they each had *something* there.

He returned to his bike and rode around the block toward the ghetto. A gloomy shadow blanketed the muddy streets, a darkness amidst the day that Pier Giorgio was not used to seeing in his beautiful city. It was as if even the sun had no desire to find its way to the homes of these people.

Ragged men stood on street corners smoking cigarettes, eyeing Pier Giorgio as he walked by. The small homes were packed tightly together and on top of one another, appearing as if they might crumble under the footsteps of a mere child. Businesses and shops looked so rundown he was unsure of which ones were open and which were closed. A group of chickens frantically fought for their lives against an attack from a stray dog, or perhaps the dog was the one fighting for his life; Pier Giorgio wasn't sure. Spindly children walked the streets without shoes or coats. In an impulsive act, Pier Giorgio took off his overcoat and wrapped it around a boy, no older than five. It was too large for him and dragged along the ground like a cape, but the boy thanked him and moved down the street.

Pier Giorgio sat down on a curb; there he stayed for an hour, lost in thought. His daze was only broken when a gentle voice came to his ears like a soft echo from a distant canyon.

"Signor, please may you spare something for me? My children have not had anything to eat in two days."

Pier Giorgio blinked and looked up. A woman covered in dirt and wearing a hole-ridden dress stood before him, holding the hands of two children dressed just as meekly.

"Pardon me, Signora, what did you say?"

"Please, may you spare something so that my children may eat today?"

"Oh, of course!" he reached down into his pockets, pulling out the wad of money his parents had given him for his high school graduation. He held out several lire.

"Thank you!" she exclaimed. "Thank you, dear sir. This is so much. We will eat for days."

She wrapped her arms around her children and ushered them away.

"Wait," he called after her. "I have more," he said, holding up the money. "What more can I give?"

"You would give me *more?*"

He hesitated. "Perhaps there are others we should help? It's best to give a little to many than much to just one family, no?"

She nodded. "Yes, of course, I'll take you to where the neediest are."

* * * * *

Back at the Frassati house, Luciana and her parents convened in their den as they waited for the servants to prepare dinner. Both adults were enjoying a drink while Luciana sat before a mirror putting on makeup.

"Where is your brother?" Adelaide asked.

"I don't know," Luciana said as she applied lipstick, smacking her lips together and admiring the color. "Up to no good, probably."

Adelaide turned to her husband who was busy reading the paper. "Alfredo, have you seen him? He promised he'd be here for dinner tonight."

"If he promised then I'm sure he'll be here," Alfredo replied without looking up from the paper.

The three of them sat in silence for a moment, until Luciana said, "Mama, after dinner may I go down to visit Teresa? She got two new dresses yesterday and claims one is too small for her, she thinks it might fit me."

"You don't need another dress," Alfredo broke in, still not glancing up from his paper. "You have hundreds upstairs."

"Oh dear, that reminds me . . ." Adelaide stopped and chuckled at the thought that had popped into her head.

"Do you remember that dress Signora Santini wore to the dinner party the other night? It was ghastly!"

Adelaide laughed again to herself.

"I do remember, but she's always lacked taste. Does it surprise you she would wear something so atrocious?"

"I suppose you're right," Adelaide agreed.

"Mama," Luciana pleaded, "you never answered. Can I go down to Teresa's after dinner and see the dress?"

"Yes, fine, just stop asking. Where is your brother, anyway?"

"I told you, I don't know."

"No one ever knows where that boy is," Alfredo echoed.

Adelaide nodded and took a sip of her drink.

* * * * *

Pier Giorgio rode out of the ghetto with empty pockets, no coat and no shoes. His bare feet hurt against the pedals, but his jumbled thoughts—those of guilt, love, inspiration, confusion, anger, and helplessness—precluded him from regarding the pain.

He was aware of the prestige in which he was raised, with servants in plenty, fine clothing, dinner parties, and a spacious, elegant home overlooking the Corso Siccardi. But suddenly the discrepancies between the life he had and those of the people he was peddling away from rose to the surface of his conscious.

He had preformed many acts of charity in the last several years, but most, in his eyes, were fleeting donations, done without enough conviction and persistence to make a difference. Something had to change. He was nearly eighteen years old and knew that manhood waited for him on the approaching horizon; a new path had to be chosen to ensure his life led toward the light of God.

He made his way over to the headquarters of the St. Vincent de Paul Society and signed up to become a full-time member. He had intended to immediately donate the money his parents had given him, but brushed off his now inability to do so, reasoning that the money had found its proper and best place.

Pier Giorgio rode back to the Cathedral in Turin and prayed before the Blessed Virgin, asking her for guidance and conviction to follow the path he suddenly felt called to follow. An urge rose within him like lava from a volcano, an urge to help the poor and any others he could. He would not merely donate his time and money here or there; he would make it his life's mission and do what he could to bring people closer to Christ.

Amidst his prayer, he glanced down at his watch and saw the hour. He fled home and burst through the door. His family was clearing away the table.

"I'm sorry, have I missed dinner?"

His mother turned away from him. "He remembers Mass times but not mealtimes," she said to no one in particular. "Such a strange boy we have."

She left for the kitchen to help the maid do the dishes, while his father strolled into his office to work for the evening. Luciana shrugged and went upstairs to her room.

Alone, Pier Giorgio went back outside and sat on the front stairs of their home, pulled out his rosary, and continued the prayers he had begun at the Cathedral.

12

Do Not Weep
for Your Children

A knock echoed throughout the tiny, two-room slum of the Costa family. Signora Costa's eyes perked, turning to her smiling children and her feeble mother resting by the fire.

"Is it him?" asked Teresina.

"I don't know, child. Why don't you run and see?"

Teresina and her brother Ettore burst from their seats at the table and ran to the door.

"Pier Giorgio!" they screamed in unison upon opening the door.

"Ah, my little friends!" he replied, smiling from ear to ear and holding a bouquet of flowers.

They jumped toward his chest to hug him but their contagious giggles brought upon his own laughter and drained his strength. They slid down his body and clung to each of his legs like little monkeys.

Signora Costa stood and greeted him. "Hello, Georgie. As you can see, we're excited for your visit."

"And I'm excited to be here," he said, entering the

house slowly and with heavy footsteps under the weight of the children. "But, I must ask; where are your beautiful children? I hear them, but I do not see them."

He playfully looked about the house, above the screaming voices and giggles below.

"Pier Giorgio! We're here! Here we are! Look down here!"

"Oh! There you two are!" He crouched down to hug them. "And these flowers are for your saintly grandmother. Won't you take them to her?"

Teresina walked them over to her grandmother.

"Thank you, dear Giorgio," Grandmother Costa said. She was unable to rise from her chair to greet him so he walked across the dark and drab room and delivered a kiss to her wrinkly cheek.

"And how are you? Getting along okay, I hope."

"Oh yes, with these children life is always sweet."

"That's my girl. And you?" he asked turning to Signora Costa. "How is your health?"

As if on cue, she coughed violently and sat back down. Pier Giorgio braced her body and got out his handkerchief for her to cough in to. When she finished, she and Pier Giorgio both noted the blood that had vomited up from her mouth, staining the white cloth with blotches of scarlet red. He quickly wrapped it up and stuffed it into his pocket before the children could see.

"Just a little cough," he said patting her back and smiling to the children. "She's fine." The worry on their faces melted away.

"What else have you brought us?" Ettore asked.

"Child, don't be so needy," his mother corrected, still clearing her throat. "Can Pier Giorgio not just come for a visit?"

"Well, as a matter of fact, I do have little gifts for you all."

The children squealed. Pier Giorgio laughed as he walked back outside to retrieve two duffle bags he had laid by the front stoop. He brought them inside and proceeded to unpack three jars of milk, two loaves of bread, candy and a board game for the children, medicine for Signora Costa, a new blanket, and a book on the writings of St. Paul for Grandmother Costa.

"This is like Christmas morning," Signora Costa exclaimed, drinking in the joy on her children's faces.

"Ah, but we are not finished yet," Pier Giorgio said. "Isn't there someone making his First Communion next week?"

"I am," Ettore said raising his hand.

"That's you?" he asked rhetorically. "Well then, these shoes must be for you!"

He pulled out brand new dress shoes, so shiny and white you could check your reflection in them.

Ettore gasped. "Those are for me?"

"Of course! You cannot receive the Lord for the first time without proper shoes to carry you to him."

Ettore grabbed the shoes and flung them on his feet. He walked around the small home, showing them off to his family.

"Take them off," his grandmother begged. "This house will ruin those immaculate shoes."

"Oh, let him enjoy them," Pier Giorgio insisted.

"Pier Giorgio," Signora Costa whispered to him as the children spoke across the room. "This is too much. What can we give you in return?"

"Nonsense. That smile is repayment enough for me."

As they watched Ettore in his new shoes, Pier Giorgio noticed a forlorn Teresina.

"And you must think I have forgotten you." A shy smile broke through her frown like sunlight through cloud cover. "Why would I forget the cutest little girl in all of *Italia*?"

"I don't know how you could," she played along.

"Have you said your prayers each night like I asked you to?" She nodded. "And do you pray for your mother? It is most important to pray for our mothers because they gave us life."

"Yes, I pray for Mama nightly, and for her to get better."

"Alright then, so you've been a good girl. That must be why God has rewarded you with a chance to go to the school with the Sisters of the Immaculate starting this fall."

Her face brightened and her jaw fell to the floor.

"Pier Giorgio," Signora Costa broke in, "how can this be?"

"Prayers are always answered," he said with a wink. "I'll take you to Sister Mary next month and she will get all your paperwork in order. We will have to get you a new dress and some new shoes as shiny as Ettore's. Are you excited?"

"Oh, yes! Yes! Thank you, Pier Giorgio!" The young girl ran and hugged him again. He swirled her around in the air and laughed. When he put her down, he noticed Signora Costa's eyes beginning to water. He changed the subject.

"Now, let's play that game I brought."

The family gathered around Pier Giorgio at the feet of Grandmother Costa so she could join in. Together they sat before the feeble flames of the fire, eating the food he had brought and playing the board game. Laughter, once an alien sound to the slum that was the Costa house, bounced off the cement walls. It was laughter that, at least for a moment, decorated the gloomy residence with the shine of a palace.

When the game was over and darkness blanketed Turin, Pier Giorgio ushered the family over to the side wall of the den, a wall completely bare, save for the crucifix he'd hung there months earlier. Even Grandmother Costa managed to rise from her chair and hobble over to stand before the fallen Son. At the sight of Pier Giorgio's head bowing, the others did as well. He led them in prayer and asked that protection be given to Signor Costa, who had died earlier that year.

Pier Giorgio helped get the children ready for bed and tucked them in, kissing them on their foreheads and assuring them he would be back in a few days. He crouched beside Ettore's ear and said, "Listen to me, young son, you can be a great help to your mother, who has such need of comfort. Do you know this?"

It was too dark to see him, but Pier Giorgio heard the movement of his head nodding against the pillowcase.

"I know you've given her trouble lately, but you must not do that; you know she's sore at heart and that is a horrible cross to bear. She needs you to be strong now that your father is gone. Yes?"

He nodded again.

Pier Giorgio rubbed his head and left the room. Signora Costa waited out in the den and walked him to the door. She led him outside and together they stood in the darkness of the ghetto. The sounds of barking dogs and men shouting at drinking taverns hovered over them.

"Pier Giorgio, I cannot thank you enough for all this. What you and the St. Vincent de Paul Society have done for me since the death of my husband is impossible to repay. I only pray the Conference will not send us another benefactor; I believe my children would die if another soul knocked on our door other than you."

He smiled. "You don't need to repay anything, Signora Costa. You may not be aware, but you and your family bring me a joy I cannot describe."

"Still, I hope my health will improve so I may try to find work."

"No, no. You must rest. Do not think about this. Your health will improve. I pray for it every day, and I know your husband does from heaven as well."

"I do hope so, but I worry that if I pass, my children will be lost amongst these mean and relentless streets. My mother will not be around much longer; if I am also gone, who will watch over them?"

"Do not weep for your children, providence will watch over them. They will grow to be strong and healthy. The Costa family shall want for nothing as long as I am here."

She hugged him so he couldn't see her tears, holding on to him for nearly a minute. When she let go, he smiled and walked away, disappearing into the darkness of the night.

13

Tears in the Darkness

Carlo laced up his shoes and slugged his way down to the first floor of his family home. He curled his head around the edge of the den wall where his parents sat listening to the chamber music playing on their record player.

"Mama, Papa, I'm off now."

They turned from their perch on the couch. "You're off to attend to your Conference duties, no?" his mother asked turning down the volume. He nodded. "Wonderful, just like your Papa many years ago." She leaned over and pinched her husband's cheek.

"And my Papa before me," Carlo's father added before taking a puff on his pipe.

Carlo rolled his eyes. "Yes, okay, well, I'm meeting Pier Giorgio and then we are set to visit one of the slums."

"Is that Alfredo Frassati's boy?" his father asked.

"Yes."

"It's surprising a boy from his stature is a member of St. Vincent de Paul."

"Which of the quarters are you visiting?" his mother asked.

"I don't know. Does it matter? They're all the same.

And trust me, Mama, Pier Giorgio will know where to go."

"Well, where are you meeting him?"

"Where else? At the Basilica della Consolata at six in the evening. He'll be there preaching; like clockwork, that one is."

Carlo waved goodbye and left the house. Outside, dusk was falling and settling calmly in the streets. It was to be a pleasant evening, one that gave way to a clear night with hundreds of stars hanging over the city like celestial lanterns. Down the block he heard the chatter and laughter of a group of young people bouncing off the café walls and awnings. He shook his head and sighed, wishing he could be a part of such laughter.

Several minutes later, the Basilica came before his line of sight. As sure as the sunrise, there stood Pier Giorgio Frassati, smiling and talking to a group of people who huddled around him as if they were suffering from hypothermia and he was a bonfire. Each of them were dressed in dowdy clothing and their skin was darkened by a layer of dirt or soot or whatever it was that gathers on the human flesh from a lack of bathing. Carlo could tell from many yards away what sort they were.

"Why do we even need to go to the slums?" he mumbled to himself. "There are plenty of downcast right here."

Carlo had yet to go on a nightly mission with Pier Giorgio to fulfill his Conference duties, but he had seen him about town in his dealings with the poor, including at this very place before the Basilica. Pier Giorgio gathered here several times a week to hand out donations and alms and speak to those who possessed a jaded spirit.

He made his way over to the crowd and listened from behind a slew of people.

"Human sorrows affect us all," Pier Giorgio said to the people before him, "but if they are seen in the light of religion, and thus of resignation, they are not harmful, but healthy, because they purify our souls from the small and inevitable stains with which we mortals so often mark them with our imperfect nature . . ."

As he went on, Carlo scanned the faces. Each hung on every word he said.

"Amazing," Carlo thought to himself, *"they cherish his words, and yet he is not yet twenty years old."*

". . . but now, my brothers and sisters, I must take my leave, for my dear friend Carlo Florio is here and we must journey across town."

At hearing his name, Carlo looked up. Pier Giorgio's eyes shone like a lighthouse in his direction, cutting across the sea of people before them. A smile stretched wide across his face, and as if by a reflection beyond his control, Carlo cast a joyous smile in return.

Pier Giorgio said his goodbyes with hugs and assurances he would be back tomorrow before hurrying to meet Carlo.

"My friend, good to see you! But we're late; shall we depart?"

Carlo nodded but hesitated when Pier Giorgio walked in the direction opposite the train station. "Should we not catch the train, Georgie?"

"No," came the simple reply, his back still to Carlo.

"But as you said, we're late."

"The money we save by walking can go to better causes."

Carlo turned back toward the street which led to the station, but realized Pier Giorgio was now almost half a block away and ran to catch up.

"How long will we be tonight?" Carlo asked when he reached him.

"I'm not sure."

Pier Giorgio's walk was brisk. Carlo struggled to keep up.

"Well, how long do you usually stay with them? You've done many benefactor visits in the past, no?"

"I have. I thought you had as well?"

"No, I just recently signed up and I'm not to go alone, yet. They said every new member should go on a call with *the* Pier Giorgio Frassati to learn what the Conference is all about, so they paired me with you tonight."

"I'm pleased to have you," Pier Giorgio said patting him on the shoulder and smiling. They paused at a street corner and waited for a break in the traffic before moving across the intersection.

"You never answered?"

"I'm sorry?"

"You never said how long you usually stay on the other side of town. I've been told you sometimes get in trouble with your parents because you return so late in the evenings."

"Have you somewhere else to be tonight, Carlo?"

He shrugged. "I considered meeting some friends from the Polytechnic, perhaps at the new restaurant in the Square in Crocetta."

Pier Giorgio glanced over to him as they continued to walk. "The amount of time I stay depends on what needs to be done. It's too hard to say."

After several more blocks spent walking in silence, Carlo took note of the change in tone on this side of the city. They had walked at least twenty blocks and moved into the shadow cast by the vibrancy from the bustling metropolis behind them. The homes and shops looked decayed, almost as if a battle had blown through the streets. He grew apprehensive for their safety as men across the street eyed them with cigarettes glued to their lips, and depression weighed upon him at the sight of a young prostitute hovering on a street corner.

"Why do you do it?" he suddenly asked.

"Why do I do what?"

"Why do you seek out the wretched and poor in these sordid corners of Turin?"

Pier Giorgio stared back blankly. "You're also here with me, are you not?"

"Yes, but only because my parents all but forced me to become a member of the Society. It's a family honor, or so they say."

They stopped yet again at an intersection. Pier Giorgio removed his worn, gray cap and ran his hand through his pitch black hair. He placed the cap back on and turned to Carlo.

"Jesus comes to me every morning in Holy Communion; I repay him in my very small way by visiting the poor."

"It's as simple as that?"

"Yes."

The intersection cleared and they moved across the street.

"Then *how* do you do it, if that's why you do it?"

"What do you mean?"

"How do you overcome your revulsion in these hovels with their foul smells? How can you be as cheery as you are when you're welcomed to these neighborhoods by a nauseating smell? I cannot even speak of what I saw on my last visit to this place, with the backed-up sewage that ran throughout the house. Or is it that you are so full of sanctity that you do not notice such conditions?"

Pier Giorgio stopped and grabbed Carlo's arm, bringing him to an abrupt halt.

"Carlo, I'm made of flesh just the same as you. If I didn't smell the odor I would not come, for there would be no reason to come. But don't ever forget that even though the house is sordid, you are approaching Christ. He told us, 'The good you do to the poor you do to Me,' did he not?"

Pier Giorgio didn't give Carlo a chance to answer.

"There is a special light behind the poor and unfortunate, one we do not have, one that has nothing to do with riches and health. I urge you to see that light tonight, not with your eyes, but with your heart."

Carlo nodded and the two set off again. Pier Giorgio curved about the corner and opened the side door of a brick building which led to an upstairs apartment resting over a bakery. Before ascending the stairs, he stopped and faced Carlo.

"We're visiting a very sick and elderly gentleman

tonight. His skin is covered in lesions and rashes and the smell you spoke of will no doubt be present. Are you sure you're alright to come with me? I don't want to force you to do something you are not able to do."

Carlo hesitated. "No, I'll come with you. I'm ready."

Pier Giorgio smiled. "I know you want to see your friends, Carlo, and there is no shame in that. But you must be mindful of a carefree life. The life of the good is the most difficult, but it is the quickest to get to heaven, and do not forget heaven should be the aspiration of us all."

Carlo considered his words.

"But even so," Pier Giorgio went on, "perhaps we will go meet your friends and smoke a cigar before the night is out; that is, if you will allow me to accompany you. I would love to make new friends. Would that be alright?"

"Yes, . . . of course."

"Wonderful!"

Pier Giorgio walked up the stairs. Carlo expected him to knock on the door, but he turned the knob slowly, cracked it open and called inside.

"Signor Cavetti, it's me, Pier Giorgio."

The smell of decayed skin blew to Carlo in the air like salt off a wave, but he moved into the apartment behind Pier Giorgio. They made their way to the back bedroom, tripping in the darkness over pots and trash scattered on the floor.

"He cannot afford electricity," Pier Giorgio whispered back to him.

Once in the room, Carlo saw a man standing in the corner peering out the window. The glow of an outside streetlamp shone into the darkness, wrapping his silhouette in a shell of light. The figure turned and spoke in a raspy voice.

"Oh, Pier Giorgio! There you are; I was looking out the window trying to note your arrival, but you have snuck past my old eyes somehow."

"I'm very crafty like that," Pier Giorgio replied laughing. He walked across the room and embraced the elderly man. Turning and wrapping his arm around the man's slumping shoulders, Pier Giorgio said, "Signor Cavetti, I want to introduce you to a dear friend who has come to visit you as well. His name is Carlo Florio."

"Oh, bless you, Carlo," the man said. He hobbled over with the help of his cane and hugged him, and though they hid in the darkness of that apartment, tears welled within Carlo's eyes.

14

Trouble Past Midnight

"Pier Giorgio! Pier Giorgio!"

From his stance on the curb, Pier Giorgio turned back toward the humming car sitting in idle.

"The paste! It's turned over!"

"What?" he asked. Pier Giorgio ran back toward the car and approached his friend, Guardia. His head was hanging out of the rolled-down window.

"This fool Tonino knocked over the pot of paste with his big feet!" Guardia exclaimed.

"It was an accident," Tonino pleaded, pushing Guardia aside.

"How will we put up the posters without the paste?" asked Giuseppe from the front passenger seat. His three friends stared at Pier Giorgio like children waiting for an answer from their father. He looked at his watch. It was nearly midnight; the market would be long closed. The political fliers for the Italian People's Party flapped in his hand as a breeze flew by.

"We'll figure something out."

He hopped into the driver's seat and jolted the clutch, speeding off around the corner of the block.

"Where are we going?" Giuseppe asked.

"We must find a restaurant or café still open," Pier Giorgio answered.

"What will that do?" Tonino asked, poking his head up to the front seat. "We're in no need of food and drink, Georgie."

"I disagree. I think a drink is *exactly* what we need after the stress you've just caused, and you're treating."

The others laughed.

"I told you, it was an accident."

"I know, Tonino, I was only joking. We'll find an open restaurant and get some flour to make more paste."

"Ah!" Giuseppe exclaimed as he followed Pier Giorgio's line of thinking. "What would we have done if ole' Georgie had not joined the I.P.P with us? A political genius, he is!"

"Yes," Guardia agreed, "and he couldn't be less of a political man. The irony is perfect!"

Pier Giorgio slowed the car to a roll and parked before Roberto's Café.

"I'll run in since I'm the one who knocked the pot over," Tonino offered. "Do we have any money to give the owner?"

"Of course not," Guardia laughed. "And you should be the last one we send in. You have no chance of persuading anyone to give us something for free."

"And why not?"

"No," Pier Giorgio broke in, "let Tonino go. He will do fine. Just tell Roberto what we need it for; he supports our cause."

Tonino jumped out of the car and ran toward the door.

"And get some water as well," Giuseppe called after him. "Flour will do us no good without water."

He disappeared into the restaurant filled with patrons huddled around small tables topped with red clothes, full plates, and glowing candlelight.

As they waited, Pier Giorgio chuckled to himself, enjoying the strange and unforeseen situation he found himself in. It had taken several conversations to convince him to join the Italian People's Party along with his friends, but after much thought, and even more prayer, he determined the cause was just.

Although the war had ended over a year ago in November of 1918, Italy was plagued by the echo of war's effects. Social unrest and class warfare brought an uneasy tension to the streets of Turin, and Pier Giorgio wanted to do what he could to help his country. He found his chance in the I.P.P., a Christian-democratic political party founded by Dr. Luigi Sturzo, a Catholic priest and leader whose example inspired Pier Giorgio. Backed by Pope Benedict XV, they posed an attractive opposition to the Italian Socialist Party because of their founding principles based on the doctrine of the encyclical letter, *Rerum Novarum*.

Still, his decision to leap into the world of politics did not come with ease.

"I don't enjoy politics," he told his friends the night he joined, "it can be a seedy business full of two-faced men. But it is the unfortunate means in which we can help the needy, and therefore it must be embraced."

But when he joined, he never imagined he would be trolling the streets of Turin in search of ingredients to make paste, all as the clock ticked past midnight.

A few minutes later, Tonino exited the restaurant empty handed and slumped back to the car.

"Roberto kicked me out," he mumbled as he climbed into the backseat. Tonino imitated the café owner in a deep, scratchy voice. "'How dare you come into my place of business asking for flour of all things, and at this hour? What's wrong with you, boy?' What's wrong with me? What's wrong with him? What a creep that man is."

Pier Giorgio chuckled. "No, Roberto is a fine man. He's only trying to run a business." He climbed out of the car and entered the café. Ten minutes later he emerged with a pitcher of water and a paper bag full of flour. The others burst into laughter and poked at Tonino. Pier Giorgio hopped in the car victoriously and chucked the bag of flour in the backseat. Tonino waved the white flag of his pride and joined in the laughter.

"How did you do it?" Guardia asked.

"I prayed to the Patron Saint of flour for intercession; Roberto stood no chance!"

They pulled down a dimly-lit side street and furiously mixed together a paste-like concoction. When they were finished, they journeyed over to the Piazza Solferino in the heart of Turin, splitting up and ornamenting the square with their posters. Nearly every inch of every monument, pole, sign, fountain, and building was adorned with the I.P.P's message and the names of their candidates.

In the midst of slapping one of his last posters up, Pier Giorgio heard a commotion just on the other side of the center fountain. A small crowd had huddled around

Tonino, questioning him rather forcefully about what he was doing.

"Oh, poor Tonino," Pier Giorgio said under his breath, "this has not been a good night for you."

Pier Giorgio and the others ran across the square and broke through the crowd. They stood alongside their friend with locked shoulders.

"What's the meaning of all this?" Guardia asked.

"Well, friends," Tonino answered, "these Socialist pigs are taking issue with the fine artwork we're putting up here in our beloved Piazza Solferino. They're not very fond of the candidates we're supporting."

"Because you Papists don't think with your heads, you think with your-"

"Our what?" Giuseppe interrupted the young man across from him. "We think with our what? Our souls? Our hearts? Oh, you may be correct, my friend, but at least we can claim to have such things."

"Just leave the adult matters up to the adults and go back to your statues of the Virgin and your bells and candles," the young man went on. "We will take care of the matter of running our country."

"Say what you will about us and our party," Pier Giorgio said stepping forward, "but speak ill of the Blessed Virgin and this night will not end well for you."

"Have you not noticed we have *double* the numbers you have?"

"Passion and faith outweigh numbers," Pier Giorgio said confidently.

Their opposition laughed. One of them went and

ripped down a sign Tonino had posted up, tearing it into many pieces only an inch before his face. Pier Giorgio grabbed Tonino's arm and pulled him back.

"It's not worth it, Tonino. Turn your cheek."

Pier Giorgio scanned the square, hoping to see a policeman on patrol. But there were only a few couples snuggling under streetlights and smoking cigarettes.

"Yes, listen to your friend," one of them said. "You men of faith cannot fight back anyway, can you?"

One of them went and tore down yet another sign. When he began to rip it up, Pier Giorgio turned back to Tonino.

"Alright, now it's worth it."

All four charged at the men standing across from them, screaming like delirious madmen! If it hadn't been such a serious and dramatic moment, Pier Giorgio might have laughed at the looks on their faces. It seemed these members of the Socialist Party were not expecting four Catholic boys to come to blows with them.

While their element of surprise helped, the fact that they were outnumbered quickly turned the tussle for the worst. The eight men regrouped and began to double team Pier Giorgio and his friends. Fists were thrown and bodies were slammed to the concrete. Giuseppe was tossed into the fountain and Pier Giorgio's shirt was ripped off. Lights flickered on in the surrounding buildings, dogs barked, and the couples under the streetlights came to watch.

The whole ordeal felt like the passing of a month, but in reality only lasted about two minutes. Pier Giorgio broke free and rounded up his friends, screaming for them to retreat before they were killed. They sprinted back to the car and jumped in, laughing hysterically despite the mad men chasing after them. The sound of screeching tires muffled the obscenities Guardia tossed out the window at their pursuers. Pier Giorgio drove like a bullet shot from a gun until he felt they were safe.

He pulled the car over and together the friends took inventory of their injuries as they laughed and relived the story, which, by no surprise, was already guilty of embellishment. By the time this story reached the others in the I.P.P, they would deserve a medal for fighting off *twenty* men from the Socialist Party.

Considering what had transpired, the friends agreed they would celebrate over a late meal and split a bottle of wine. By the time Pier Giorgio made his way home the sunlight was approaching the edge of the Turin horizon. He tiptoed inside and got ready for bed, but fell to his knees as he always did before climbing under the covers. With the familiar string of beads sliding between his fingers, he thanked the Virgin Mother for protecting him and his friends on such a wild evening.

Not two months later he prayed to her once again by his bedside, thanking her for the election of 100 members of the I.P.P to the Italian Parliament.

15

Our Lady of Oropa

Pier Giorgio awoke at dawn. The first glimmers of sunlight filtered through the window and crept across his face, turning the darkness beneath his eyelids to crimson. A smile found his face as he listened to the chirping of the birds outside.

"What a glorious day this will be," he whispered to himself.

He leapt from bed and quickly changed, dressing himself for the long hike into the mountains of northern Italy. He packed his rucksack full of food and supplies and scribbled a note to his family:

Dear Papa, Mama and Luciana,

What a special day for our family! I cannot wait to experience the crowning of Our Lady at the shrine in Oropa. I'm simply too excited to wait and plan to hike there. I know you will be traveling by car, but I will look for you this afternoon! I love you!

Pier Giorgio

He crept out of the house without a sound and headed north from Pollone. The journey before him consisted of a rugged climb roughly eight kilometers long and rising some 2,000 feet higher above sea level. The year had progressed deep into autumn and the air was brisk, with thick clouds rolling atop the mountains signaling the arrival of snow.

Up and up he climbed, letting the sounds of the civilized world be swept away in the swirling winds of the Alps. He fell into a zone of prayer, taking each careful step with an uncanny instinct for climbing. His fingers blindly navigated their way over the flower seeds he had strung around fishing wire—a rosary gift he would often make and give to the poor he helped. His whispered prayers ascended into the atmosphere like incense, fertilizing the soil of heaven and giving life to the roses blooming at the Virgin Mother's feet.

He paused for lunch on the bank of a steep hill but ate little, only a few sips of water from his thermos and a can of soup. It would be the only meal he ate that day, adhering to a fast he'd set for himself in honor of the coming ceremony at Our Lady of Oropa.

After finishing he set off again, climbing through a hazy mist that stealthily moved across the mountains and clouded his vision. His prayers increased as his eyes began to fail him and he became worried he would not make it in time at such a slow pace. Peering through the mist, he humored himself by imagining these were the welcoming clouds of heaven and he was on the threshold of paradise.

"I should be so lucky," he said to himself with a chuckle. "But my mountains are the next best thing."

When the mist thinned, a light snow began to fall. He buttoned up his coat, pulled a wool toboggan down over his messy hair, and marched onward. Each snow-flake swirled down, all unique from the others, and caked the ground, leaving a thin layer of soft ice that crunched beneath his footsteps. At times he had to use his ice pick to gain traction and continue the climb higher into the mountains.

An alpine forest signaled the approach of the shrine. He recognized the pines and silver furs surrounding the area of which he had climbed to several times before. With an hour to spare before the celebratory Mass, he came into view of the arched dome nestled in the mountains around it. Tall pillars rose beneath the dome bracing the roof of the church. The granite structure blended naturally into the autumn forest and mountains behind it, appearing as if God had formed it with His very hands.

Pier Giorgio stood resting beneath the branches of a spruce pine which caught the fluttering snow before it landed atop his head. He let his eyes drink in the sight before him and thanked St. Eusebius, who had discovered the Black Madonna statue in Jerusalem. It was said to have been carved by St. Luke the Evangelist, and returned it to the small hermitage in these mountains. Throughout the years dozens of miracles had been attributed to the small statue which now sat in a chapel in the church before Pier Giorgio.

He sprinted forward with a burst of adrenaline and made his way through the small town of Oropa. Others were arriving for the ceremony and the streets were packed full of pilgrims. He wanted to search for his family but there was no time; he was set to serve at the Mass. Pier

Giorgio made his way up to the church and found the back room where the other altar boys were preparing.

Throughout the next two hours Pier Giorgio felt as if he was floating. The outside world disappeared and a joy shone from his face that seemed ethereal to those around him. He marched among the procession, led by an Italian Cardinal, toward the six-foot tall Black Madonna. He watched with wondrous eyes when the Cardinal placed the crown on top of the statue; the third crown, as it was, which now rested atop the ones placed there in previous centuries by other Popes and Cardinals.

After the ceremony, he searched in vain for his family amidst the chaos of pilgrims, but no matter where his eyes looked, he could not find them.

* * * * *

The café bustled with activity—chatter, laughter, the clinging of utensils against porcelain plates and the banging of pots and pans back in the kitchen. Luciana sat at a table with her parents and their friends.

"Mama?" she pleaded.

Adelaide was engaged in another conversation, ignoring her daughter.

"Mama . . . ?"

"You must come the next time we have everyone over, Maria," she said to the woman sitting next to her. "I'll show you some of my pieces."

Before the woman could answer, Luciana said again, "Mama?"

"What, child?" Adelaide finally said turning to her.

"May I leave now? My friends are meeting up toward the chapel."

"Fine, yes, but come back soon. We leave in an hour to return home." Adelaide turned back to the woman. "My apologies. I'm afraid these young children today have no manners," she added with a defensive chuckle.

Luciana rolled her eyes before rising and leaving the café.

"You have wonderful children," Maria answered. "That Pier Giorgio, what a handsome fellow he is. You must need full-time security at the house to keep the girls away."

"They do dote on him," she said proudly.

"Too bad he'll never be able to marry one of those girls," Dino, Maria's husband, interjected into the women's conversation. He turned away from Alfredo, whom he had been talking to.

"And why not?" Adelaide asked.

"Because everyone knows your boy is going to become a priest!"

Dino laughed.

"My boy will not be a man of the cloth," Alfredo quickly replied, "he'll be following in my footsteps at the paper."

"Yes," Adelaide agreed, "he'll carry on the family business."

Dino took a large swig of wine, put it down and shook his head as he swallowed. "No, no, the only family business he'll carry on is the business of the Holy Family," he said laughing again at himself.

"Dino, you've had too much wine," Maria said moving his glass away from him.

"Nonsense," he fought back, taking it from her. He

looked back to Alfredo. "Everyone sees him around Turin, always with a rosary in hand, going in and out of the Cathedral each hour. My boy said he'd been talking about this ceremony for weeks. 'His Madonna' was to receive her crown, he claimed."

"I have no problem with my boy respecting the Faith," Alfredo claimed, "but I assure you he'll be joining us at *La Stampa* in just a few short years. If you need someone to absolve you from your horrible sins, Dino, you'll have to find another man to do it. I'll not have my son become a priest for many reasons, the most of which is not to subject him to hearing your confessions."

Dino laughed, as did Alfredo and the two women. Dino and Maria nestled close to one another amidst their laughter, sneaking in a kiss and enjoying the wine overtaking their senses and the cheerful mood of the café.

Alfredo snuck a glance over to his wife, and she at him. Their smiles faded; they both knew the other was feigning amusement. Adelaide fidgeted in her seat as Alfredo flagged down their server. When she approached, he held up his wine glass, "Another."

She nodded and headed back toward the kitchen. Alfredo waited impatiently for her to return.

* * * * *

Finally, Pier Giorgio spotted Luciana standing in front of the church.

"Luciana!" he called out running toward her. He nearly tackled her when he threw his arms around her, causing her friends to chuckle and leave.

"Georgie, I was in the middle of a conversation."

"Did you see? Did you see the ceremony?"

"No."

"No? What do you mean?

"I mean, 'no'."

"Where were you? Where are mama and papa?"

"They're down at the café in town with their friends," she said, looking more interested in people watching than the conversation with her brother.

"Did they see the ceremony? Were they at the Mass?"

"No, we ate down there. But I had to leave; it was all very boring, all their adult-talk. It was nice being with my friends, until you scared them away . . ."

"How could you all skip it?" he asked.

"Georgie, you know they didn't come up here for the ceremony; they came to socialize, to 'see and be seen,' as they say. They dragged me with them to the café. I'd have come with you to the ceremony if I could've."

Pier Giorgio's gaze fell to the ground, his expression lost. Luciana went back to watching the many people pass by, mostly the boys.

"Well, I suppose we should walk down and meet them," she finally said. "Are you coming?"

Pier Giorgio remained lost in thought.

"Georgie?"

"Yes?"

"I'm going to find Mama and Papa. Are you going to come? We're leaving soon."

"Oh, yes, perhaps I'll come in a moment. I want to see the Madonna one more time."

"Do what you must."

After she had disappeared into the crowd, Pier Giorgio returned his focus to the chapel behind him. Most of the pilgrims had left and were headed back down the mountain. As they walked down, Pier Giorgio cut through them, walking back up.

He moved slowly into the chapel, as he always did when he entered a church. It felt wrong to enter in a rush. In moving slowly, he could prepare himself to meet the Divine.

Once inside, his body was drawn to the statue like metal to a magnet. He fell to his knees and prayed fervently, asking that his parents be filled with the faith that he so treasured. Tears gathered in his eyes as he peered up at the Black Madonna adorned in a golden robe and crowns, holding the child Jesus in her arms. But he fought back the tears and felt the burning in his throat that comes from swallowing such emotions.

Without taking note of the time, hours passed. He rose and found his way down into the town of Oropa, now all but deserted. His parents and sister must have left. Among the darkness of the night he could not hike back to Pollone, so he rented a room at the humble inn. There he prayed the Rosary for the third time that day, kneeling on the cold, stone ground. From his prayers he gained comfort over his sadness, the sorrows he felt for his parents', and even now his sister's, tepid faith. He prayed for a change within them, within their hearts.

As it was, a change was coming for Pier Giorgio, but it was a change he could've never seen coming.

16

Goodbye to *Italia*

Pier Giorgio walked out of the Teatro Regio di Torino humming to himself, reliving the opera scene by scene. Walking out of such an artistic performance sent shivers of inspiration through his spirit, and as he turned down the block he broke into song, piercing the night air with his off-balanced tones and howling at the full moon above like a wild wolf. A group of girls strolling by giggled at his antics.

"Ah, Signoras," he faced them and said, "I see you were admiring my singing. And may I now offer to serenade you further with poems from my beloved Dante?"

They laughed again, their giggles as high-pitched as tea kettles.

One of them asked, "Who is this boy?"

"Boy?" he piped. "Signora, I am clearly a *man*. And my name is Pier Giorgio Frassati. It's a pleasure to meet you all!"

"I know your name," another one said.

"I hope it is a name you've heard fond things about."

"Yes," another one agreed, "my Papa speaks of your Papa regularly. He owns *La Stampa*, no?"

"That he does! My Papa is a fine man, and clearly your father is an educated man."

"I know your name because I go to the Royal Polytechnic," the fourth one offered.

"Yes!" Pier Giorgio exclaimed. "I knew your pretty face was familiar." She blushed as red as the sunset. "You are in the *Gaetana Agnesi*," he went on, "the sisterly organization to our Catholic men's club at the University. I'm an avid member of the *Cesare Balbo*."

"I have heard you are," she confirmed with a flirtatious smile. "We're going down to the Square to meet more of our friends, would you care to join us?" She batted her lashes and twirled her long, black hair with her finger. Her friends playfully poked at her back, pushing her toward Pier Giorgio, whose confidence was beginning to dissolve into boyish jitters.

"Oh . . . well, thank you for the invitation." His jovial expression faded but was quickly replaced by a forced and polite smile. He glanced at his watch even though he knew he was already late. "Unfortunately, I have another commitment I must be off to. But perhaps I will see you in my dreams, no?"

They laughed again and departed down the street. He watched them walk away until they fell from sight around the corner, admiring the femininity and beauty of their elegant walks. He sighed, took a step after them, paused, then turned in the other direction.

He raced across town to a poverty-stricken quarter on the northwest side of Turin. There, standing beneath a flickering streetlight, he saw his friend, Father Robotti, smoking a cigarette and sipping on a flask.

"Hey," he called out, "is it not a sin for a priest to sneak in a few sips of brandy on a Saturday night?"

Father Robotti turned and smiled, stuffing his flask back in his overcoat pocket. He quickly dropped the cigarette and squashed the butt with his shoe, then put his hands in his pockets, rocked on his heels, and whistled toward the sky to infer his innocence.

"No, no, I saw you," Pier Giorgio said upon reaching him.

They laughed and embraced. The priest was tall and dressed in his black robe. He wasn't old, perhaps ten years Pier Giorgio's senior, but his hair was already charcoal gray; no doubt, Pier Giorgio mused, from the stress of being a priest.

"Dear Georgie, you won't tell the old ladies in our parish, will you? I can enjoy a smoke and a quick drink in these mean streets without the glare of judgmental eyes, but if word gets back home to the affluent districts I might be in for some trouble with the Bishop."

"Why don't we just say you were drinking some black coffee?"

"Ah, if only that were true. You were right the first time; brandy is my weakness."

"We all have our weaknesses, Father. I'm sure the Lord sees the work you're doing in these downtrodden neighborhoods anyhow."

They surveyed the dark and broken streets, littered with seedy men and somber women mulling around. Their lifeless faces were void of hope or purpose.

"To be honest, Georgie, I needed a little courage from my brandy to enter this neighborhood. Each time I come I'm not so sure I'll ever see my pillow again. I thank you for answering my call to accompany me. It's a sad day in our country when a priest must hire a young friend to serve as a bodyguard, especially when he cannot trust the police."

"It's nothing, Father. I'm glad to come escort you to visit these homes."

"But you are a young man on a Saturday night. Had you no plans?"

"No, Father. I was able to see the opera in the early evening, but nothing else. Let us be on our way."

They walked further into the slums, passing by homes thrown together with pieces of large tin and rotted wood. Amidst these hollows, and all over the city, for that matter, people had begun to revolt against one another in the power vacuum that had come about since the end of the war. A clash of ideals concerning the future of post-war Italy brought chaos and tension to the streets. Italy in 1920 was not the same country Pier Giorgio had come to love in his youth.

Father Robotti looked over and eyed Pier Giorgio suspiciously, as if investigating him.

"You're not afraid to enter these streets, are you?"

He shook his head. "If you come to someone in the name of Christ, you can never be afraid."

The priest chuckled. "Said very well, Georgie."

"I think the work you're doing trying to ease the political tension of our city is very important and I'm glad to help. I know there have been dozens of strikes and demonstrations recently, and even blood has been shed. This all has to stop."

"It may not stop until those who are striking and demonstrating get nationalization of the public utilities, among their many other demands."

Father Robotti glanced down at the I.P.P badge pinned in the buttonhole of Pier Giorgio's coat.

"You are proud to wear that badge, no?"

"Indeed. I know it can attract angry stares from our political opponents. My own mother has asked that I not wear it out of the house during this time of social unrest, but the whole point of a badge is to show one's allegiance. How strong is your allegiance if you only wear it in the darkness of your own home? And anyway, I find it serves as a springboard to discuss the I.P.P's cause of justice for the poor and leadership focused on our Faith."

"And did the badge serve you well when you visited the metallurgic factory at Borgo Dora last month and put a stop to that riot?"

Pier Giorgio glanced over but did not answer.

"Yes," the priest went on, "I heard about that. How were you able to walk into that factory with *that* badge on and convince them to suppress their violence? I have to imagine there were many opponents of the I.P.P there."

Pier Giorgio shrugged. "Perhaps."

"How were you able to keep them from ripping you apart, then? I must know."

"A fair question," he replied smiling, "but the Lord was with me. I suppose I'll have to give him the credit."

"Well, let us pray you have brought your talent for

peace tonight. We'll be entering many homes, several of which are the leaders of the demonstrations occurring each night in the streets. I hope to urge them toward peace, or our beloved country could be torn apart by civil war."

"I'll be by your side all night."

Their eyes met and Father Robotti nodded, suddenly filled a strong sense of courage. For the next three hours the two of them knocked on the doors of some of the most notorious instigators of violence in their city, men who had poked the fires of civil unrest throughout the last year. Father Robotti and Pier Giorgio urged them to work peacefully with their opposition and made plans to deliver food and other alms to their community the following week. These acts of kindness softened the hard edges and bitter scars of these gruff men.

Pier Giorgio often let Father Robotti do the talking, but found a way to set the room at ease when he spent their visits playing with the children in the corner of the small homes. Many of them already knew him from his past visits to their slums.

At the end of the evening he escorted Father Robotti home safely, and having fulfilled his duty, headed home. His steps were made lightly and without care, energized from the successful evening he had shared with the priest.

But upon entering the house, he heard the muffled cries of his sister coming from the den. He hurried down the hall to see his father sitting on the couch, rubbing his sister's back. His mother was on the other side of the room pouring herself a drink from their wet bar.

"What's happened?" He quickly entered the room and took off his coat, throwing it over a nearby chair and approaching his crying sister.

"Where have you been?" his mother fired back. "It's very late."

"I . . . I was out with friends."

"Are you sure you were not out gathering subscriptions for *Il Momento* again?" his father questioned. "Do you know how embarrassing it is for me to go to work and tell my employees my son is working for our rival paper?"

"Please, Papa, it doesn't have to be them against you. I'm sorry if I have offended you. I told you this already."

"Everything in this country is one against the other right now, Georgie. They are the paper of the Popular Party, and we are that of the Liberal Party. You should know this. If you are with them, then you can go to *Il Momento* if you're hungry for dinner. Perhaps they will take you in."

"Are you surprised our son adopted the cause of that paper?" Adelaide asked, looking at no one in particular and gazing out the nearby window. "Every young, Catholic boy at the Polytechnic is working for them."

Pier Giorgio changed the subject. "Can someone please tell me why Luciana is weeping?" he asked sitting down beside her.

"Papa is making us move to Germany," she blurted out amidst her sobs.

"What?" he asked in disbelief.

"Your father has been asked to become the Italian Ambassador to Germany," his mother clarified. "Prime Minister Giolitti has given his blessing; your father leaves next week and we will join him at the end of this month in Berlin."

"That . . . that can't be. What will . . . when?"

"Your mother just told you, at the end of this month."

"But my exams for school are next month."

"Then you will stay with Aunt Elena until your studies are over," his father answered nonchalantly. "She will be here at the house while we're gone."

"How long will you hold this position, Papa?"

"There's no way to know. At least a year or two."

Pier Giorgio fought back tears as he considered this dramatic upheaval of his life and what he would leave behind—the friends, churches, classes, and many causes he was so invested in.

"It will be good for our family to get out of this crazed city for a while, don't you think, Adelaide?" Alfredo asked his wife.

She didn't answer, but rather continued to stare out the window into the darkness and sip on her drink.

"I don't want to leave my friends," Luciana bemoaned.

"You'll make new friends, and we'll be living in the very luxurious Italian Embassy. I promise you will love it, Luciana."

Her head perked and she wiped at her nose. "How luxurious?"

"Very," her father answered with a smile.

Pier Giorgio swallowed hard and walked over to his father, extending his hand.

"Congratulations, Papa. You continue to amaze us all with your accomplishments and achievements."

Alfredo accepted his son's hand and the two hugged.

The family built a fire and huddled in the den as they discussed the new life awaiting them in Germany. Luciana gradually warmed to the idea of living in a foreign place as Alfredo described the state dinners they would host and the many attractions to see in Berlin. He framed it as an adventure, and all the while Pier Giorgio displayed a sense of happiness to appease his father, but inside his heart ached for the homeland he would leave behind.

17

An Influential Meeting

Pier Giorgio wrapped the striped tie around his neck and looped it within itself, forming a loose knot just beneath his chin. He surveyed his work in the mirror and found it adequate. He grabbed his dark blue sport coat from the bed and threw it over his torso, completing his formal attire for the embassy dinner.

Downstairs he could already hear people arriving for the party as the servants ran recklessly about the house making their final preparations. The noises might have been odd in a normal house, but such sounds had become as constant as the hum of a heater at the Frassati's new home in Berlin. There was never a shortage of political guests visiting his father, in addition to the hired help who seemed to work round the clock.

He took a deep breath, surveyed his reflection in the mirror again, and headed for his bedroom door. When he opened it, he saw Luciana across the hall in her own room struggling to hook a glittery necklace beneath the long hair layering the back of her neck.

"Oh, Georgie, won't you help me with this?" She walked across the hall and turned so he could hook the clasp of the diamond necklace. Once completed, she faced him, smiling as brightly as her necklace shone in the light of the hallway chandelier. Her black sequin dress fell to the floor, covering even her feet.

"So, how do I look?"

"Marvelous," came his reply, though without much effort.

"You could be more convincing."

"I just cannot help wondering how much that necklace costs."

"I don't know, but *nothing* for me to wear it tonight, so no lectures. It's a temporary gift from the German government. Who am I to turn them down?"

"It seems they like to shower Papa with gifts each week. They must want to impress something upon him."

"Perhaps, but mother and I may as well enjoy these doting gifts while we can, no? You could too, if you wanted to. Oh, Georgie," she said reaching out to fiddle with the knot of his tie. "Why must you always wear your ties so crooked?"

She took his hand and dragged him over to the mirror of his mahogany bureau. She forced him to crouch so she could stand behind him and wrap her arms around his broad shoulders, straightening and tightening the knot. She stood for a moment admiring her brother's reflection.

He was taller than most boys, but not awkwardly, with robust arms formed and strengthened from all his mountain climbing. His hair was usually unkempt but met his forehead in a harmonious line which curved down at its midpoint. His eyes were dark but full of vitality and were encompassed by long, curly lashes. His skin was darker than hers and his teeth straighter and whiter, but he hid his good looks behind his humility, and for this she could never resent him.

She continued to stare long after the tie knot was pulled tight.

"What?" he asked innocently.

She smiled. "Just thinking how handsome my older brother is."

"Don't flatter me with such lies."

"I wouldn't be surprised if there are several beautiful, young women here tonight, Georgie. You should make yourself known and available. Use such a fancy occasion and our father's good name to introduce yourself."

"Don't hold your breath. I'm waiting for the right Italian girl to come along, one I don't anticipate meeting in Berlin tonight."

He loosened his tie with a grin. She huffed and rolled her eyes.

Together they descended the stairs with their arms locked. He had hoped she would remain by his side for the remainder of the evening, but within seconds she broke off into a conversation with her mother and several diplomats. Pier Giorgio tried to assimilate into the group but found the exchange about the latest automobile to hit the market rather dull. A joke was offered by a stout man with a white and curly mustache and the group burst into laughter; Pier Giorgio forced a detached chuckle and quietly excused himself from the conversation. No one noticed.

He floated from room to room, picking at some of the

food and avoiding any eye contact that would bait him into a discussion with one of his father's acquaintances. An instrument trio played music from the drawing room and for a while he enjoyed their melodies as he surveyed a large globe in the corner of the room. He placed his finger on the map and spun the sphere with closed eyes, stopping it and imagining a new life in the location his finger determined at random.

After an hour, he noticed the embassy chancellor, Rofi, walking into the kitchen to check on the food. Pier Giorgio followed him and asked for several loaves of bread and some cans of soup.

"What do you need these for?" asked Rofi, pointing to the maid to bring him Pier Giorgio's requests.

"I want to take them across town to an area I read about in the paper. I have determined they'll need these items more than our dinner guests."

"Which area?"

"Alexanderplatz."

The cooks, maids and butlers glanced at each other with veiled eyes.

"Why on earth would the son of the Italian Ambassador journey into such a place?" Rofi asked.

"To deliver bread and soup. Did my request not make this clear?"

Rofi surveyed the other faces in the room. He grabbed the bag of food from the maid and ushered Pier Giorgio towards the door. He spoke in a whisper, muffling his voice from the hired help behind them.

"Son, you should not go to such a place, at least not at

night. This area is nothing but misery."

"That's why I *should* go there," Pier Giorgio replied, taking the burlap bag full of food from him. He headed toward the back door to avoid his departure causing a scene. "Tell my Papa I'm upstairs ill with fever if he asks where I am."

"What if he checks on you?"

"He won't." Pier Giorgio paused and grabbed a bouquet of flowers resting in a vase of water by the door, shaking the dripping water over the sink. "Thank you, Rofi, and everyone else. The Lord smiles upon your gifts to the people of Alexanderplatz."

The night was cold. His breath emerged in a cloud of fog behind his chattering teeth as he wondered how much longer the lingering winter of 1921 would last before spring brought forth warmer weather. The sounds of a Berlin Saturday night clamored about him—car horns honking, buses barreling by, pedestrians filling the streets, and music playing at a nearby bar. He stopped and looked at a map he had slid into his pocket before leaving. Once certain he was traveling in the right direction, he set out toward the slums he sought.

The neighborhood of Alexanderplatz was a collection of ghettos stacked together, overflowing with an assortment of deprived and pitiable souls. The war had rushed its way through Germany and caused the destruction of not just buildings and homes, but hope and faith. Refugees from Russia had migrated west in search of a place outside the curtain of the Communist Revolution, but upon settling in the German capital, work, food, and shelter were as foreign to them as their new city.

Germans themselves were hit hard by the war reparations imposed by the Treaty of Versailles, devaluing their currency to the precipice of irrelevance. A large portion of their population was reduced to poverty as they flocked to boarding houses and fell into trenches of despair.

It was an odd thing, but Pier Giorgio felt at home for the first time in Berlin the moment he stepped into the crumbled streets of Alexanderplatz. It reminded him, in a sort of nostalgic way, of the downtrodden neighborhoods of Turin.

He considered how the wealthy had a myriad of distinctions between them—the style of their mansions, the type of automobiles they drove, where they vacationed, what sort of leisure they enjoyed, and all the like—while the poor had but one focus: *survival.* This dependence on a will to make it through each day while fending off thirst, hunger, and the natural elements, unified them across the globe into a common cause, and it was this unified feeling and focus on survival upon which Pier Giorgio thrived.

The distractions of the material world were like barnacles clinging to the soul, slowing down one's journey to God. But the poor, without such diversions of pleasure, kept their focus straight ahead; they had no other option but to place their hope in the Lord. He found the poor, sick, and disabled to be like fallen leaves scattered about the ground in late autumn; while some saw them as a nuisance, he was charmed by their presence.

Pier Giorgio fell into the gutters of Alexanderplatz and bounced from hovel to hovel as if he had resided there all

his life, introducing himself with a radiant smile and handing out donations from his bag like ole' St. Nick himself.
Residents emerged from their cold and hollow homes,
astounded by the charity waiting for them at their doors.
Each visit varied, from those who wanted no part of his
company but gladly accepted the food, to those who welcomed him in and hugged him before his departure. The
elderly woman he handed the flowers to even kissed him
square on the lips.

Once he was out of supplies he continued to navigate
the dark ghettos, giving away his socks, shoes and a coat
to a homeless man. He may have ultimately returned to
the Italian Embassy just as the dinner guests were leaving,
naked as the day he was born, if he were not more prudent
with his charity.

But before leaving the neighborhood something caught
his attention in the distance. A man dressed in black was
mirroring Pier Giorgio's own actions. A priest, it would
seem from where Pier Giorgio stood, was also dolling out
goods and supplies. Pier Giorgio, drawn to him and his
altruistic actions, began to follow the man.

It would have been quite common for Pier Giorgio to
walk up to this priest and introduce himself, as his gre-
garious nature had always allowed him the comfort and
privilege to do such things, but something held him back.
He enjoyed watching this priest and his interactions with
the poor. And so Pier Giorgio continued to shadow him,
staying some yards back and hopping from block to block.

It was nearly an hour later when, not realizing his nearing proximity to the one he was spying upon, the priest

whipped his body around and took ten aggressive steps toward a dumbfounded Pier Giorgio.

"What is it, boy?" he screamed. "What do you want? You'll not rob this priest, I assure you!"

Pier Giorgio stumbled back and tripped over a crack in the sidewalk, falling to his backside.

"Signor," he pleaded from the ground, "I mean, Father, no! I have no intention of robbing you."

"What do you want, then?"

"To . . . to meet you, I suppose."

"What?"

"To make your acquaintance."

The man waited a moment, as if sizing up the young Italian's true intentions, then stuck out his hand and helped him to his feet. Pier Giorgio dusted himself off and took in the man's face for the first time. He was middle-aged, with worn skin and a powerful jaw. His eyes were a rich blue that shone in the streetlamp above them, and his blonde hair hung down beneath the hat atop his head.

"Well, why didn't you just come say so instead of hovering in the shadows?"

"I'm not exactly sure."

The priest eyed him up and down.

"So then, what's your name? And where might I ask are your shoes? You're either insane or an idiot for walking around these streets barefoot on a cold night like this."

Pier Giorgio smiled with the realization that he was going to love this grumpy priest.

18

Finding Clarity

Father Carl Sonnenschein was a man of action. He was a passionate Catholic, one filled with vigor, and a man who applied a blunt approach to the spreading of the Faith. He reversed the roles in the relationship between the Church and her threats, acting as a predator rather than a prey, attacking and cutting off all heresies and injustices before they could blossom. Around Berlin he was well-respected, even by those outside the Catholic Church. He embraced a life of poverty in order to combat it for others, working tirelessly in the ghettos of Berlin. His actions had earned him the moniker, "the Saint Francis of Berlin."

Father Carl was born in Düsseldorf, Germany in 1876 and earned an education not only in the priesthood, but also in sociology, a rare combination for his time. His studies took him all the way to Rome, where he had a profound effect on the Italian Catholics establishing the Popular Union in 1906.

Once back in Germany, he held the role of the chief organizer of the German Catholic Movement and went on to establish the General Office of Labor, the Catholic People's University, the Catholic Artists' Club, and even found time to act as the editor of Berlin's Catholic newspaper. He made a concerted effort to promote the foundation of Catholic student clubs in all the universities of Germany, breeding faith into students, teachers, and workers alike.

In short, he was Pier Giorgio's hero.

The two took to each other quickly, becoming as inseparable as salt and seawater. Pier Giorgio thrived on Father Carl's example and soaked in his spiritual nourishment like a sponge. They made quite the pair, despite their conflicting personalities. Pier Giorgio could make conversation with a willow tree and bring life to its drooping branches, while Father Carl seemed to shy away from common human interaction. Yet both possessed a pure spirit and a desire to spread the Faith, and it was this inner flame that united them.

After meeting Father Carl, Pier Giorgio settled into his new place in Berlin. He still journeyed back to Turin at times to further his progress for his mining degree, and he took family vacations to Pollone. But for the most part he spent the next year entrenched in his new life amongst the Germans. He grew to love them, cherishing their spirit despite the difficult lot they had been cast from the repercussions of the Great War.

This was a vital time in his life, a moment where his path came to a fork he could not ignore. Despite continuing on with his university studies in Mining Engineering and serving the poor as a layman, the call of a priestly vocation still lingered within his soul. It was like a mountain in the distance he yearned to climb, but he was unsure of the valley awaiting him on the other side. It was not that he feared what awaited him; rather, he was hesitant if that was what God wanted from him. It was through his experiences with Father Carl that clarity came, though not in the fashion he anticipated such clarity to come.

On a summer night, journeying through the streets of Berlin on their way to deliver several jugs of clean water to a boarding house, the two of them mused about their favorite religious texts.

"Saint Paul is the father of the written word, as far as I'm concerned," Pier Giorgio said confidently. "I wrote down a copy of his *Hymn to Charity* and carry it around with me at all times; it's in my wallet at this very moment. The wisdom from his pen has altered the path of many souls."

"You'll get no argument from me there," Father Carl agreed, "but saying Saint Paul is your favorite religious author is like telling me the sunset over the Adriatic is splendid; such statements are too obvious to be interesting. I was looking for something more original from you, Georgie."

"But the sunset over the Adriatic *is* splendid. The truth should not be taken for granted, Father Carl; it is anything but obvious during these troubled times."

Father Carl chuckled but nodded in agreement.

They turned a corner toward a dark alley which led to the boarding house some blocks over. A rain storm had pushed through the area and the summer moonlight reflected in the many puddles gathered in the dips of the street. Pier Giorgio hopped over each one as if he were playing hopscotch, while Father Carl trudged through them without thought.

But once halfway down the street, a door from the adjacent building burst open with a loud thud, as if someone had kicked it open. Two burly men emerged with a young woman thrown over their shoulders. Her body was limp and her face lifeless. Inside the building and beyond the open door, the bustling sounds of a crowded taproom flooded the once-quiet alley. They laid the woman on the ground not two yards from the feet of Pier Giorgio and Father Carl. Upon seeing the two unexpected strangers in the alley, they grunted and walked back inside.

The woman, meanwhile, lay on the wet street on the verge of unconsciousness, lost in the recesses of her self-inflicted darkness. She moaned and tried to move, but lacked the strength. She was young, dressed all in black, and quite grimy in appearance, as if she had not bathed in quite some time.

Father Carl and Pier Giorgio rushed to the woman and lifted her up, dragging her over to the nearby curb. Pier Giorgio held her up as Father Carl ran to retrieve their jugs of water. He removed the cork of one and tilted her head back.

"Come on there, girl," Father Carl urged, pouring water onto her lips, "talk to us. Wake up. Tell us your name. Where do you live?"

She moaned again before vomiting in the street. The two of them held her firmly and waited for her to finish. They poured some water on her face and helped her take a few more sips. Pier Giorgio noted a tattoo on her neck, seemingly of a dragon. He wondered why someone would get such a thing painted on her body.

For twenty minutes they sat with her, but nothing could bring the girl back from the stupor of her inebriation, precluding them from determining a place they could take her.

"What should we do, Father Carl?"

"We cannot leave her."

"No, but we cannot take her to the boarding house. It's one only for men, no?"

The priest nodded. "You're right; it wouldn't be safe for her. You never know what men could be there. Some may be of the dangerous sort, especially to a woman in this state."

"What then?"

Father Carl thought for a moment more, then said, "Come, we must carry her."

They lifted her up, balancing her between them and each taking a jug of water in their other hand. Father Carl gave directions and together they moved her slowly, ten blocks to the east. Pier Giorgio never asked where they were going, trusting in Father Carl.

But as they crossed block after block, Pier Giorgio wondered if this situation would draw curious eyes. A priest carrying a young, drunk, and defenseless woman through the streets would surely attract the ire of any they passed, would it not? But he didn't note any such stares and judgments, finding most of the people to be disinterested, or even possibly understanding.

Finally, they stopped before a small, stone home. It was one story, with a thatched roof, wooden door, and two windows on either side glowing with light. It was an old home, but Pier Giorgio thought it quite cozy.

Father Carl handed the girl, now completely lost to the blackness, over to Pier Giorgio, who scooped her up in his arms and remained perched on the narrow walk over-run by grass and weeds. Father Carl knocked on the door and a minute later an elderly man dressed in plaid pajamas arrived at the doorway hunched over his cane.

"Tobias, my dear friend, thank God you're home."

"Father Carl, where else would an old man be at this hour other than at his home? What brings you here? What's the matter?"

"My friend and I were on a nightly mission," he said turning toward Pier Giorgio behind him and holding out his hand, "but we came across this young woman who has had far too much to drink. We don't know where to take her."

The elderly man knew what was being asked of him.

"Yes, of course, bring her in."

He waved them into his home and led them down a narrow hallway adorned with family photos to a small den. A couch rested before a window overlooking the back-yard. At Tobias's prompting, Pier Giorgio softly laid the girl down. Tobias instructed them to bring him a towel, an empty bucket, and a glass of water. Within minutes he was dabbing her forehead with a damp cloth and feeding her sips of water.

"She's fine," Tobias assured them. "Carry on with your mission. I'll see that she finds her way home tomorrow."

"Are you sure you're alright with her?" Pier Giorgio asked.

"No one can nurse a hangover better than me," Tobias claimed. "Isn't that right, Father Carl?"

Father Carl cracked a knowing smile. "I brought Tobias this woman because he is trustworthy, but I'm familiar with the weaknesses of his youth, and something tells me he may be an expert in how to help her come out of the stupor of her current state."

Tobias laughed so hard his chest collapsed and sent him into a coughing fit. He possessed the distinct sound of raspy phlegm clogging his lungs which so many smokers held claim to. Though a sincere man, Pier Giorgio saw years of bad habits hanging off him.

Father Carl thanked Tobias and a moment later he and Pier Giorgio had left the home. Again they set out for the boarding house with their jugs of water, an hour removed from their intended itinerary. They found the long, rectangular-shaped building they sought, an old war bunker converted into a house for the homeless, and delivered the water. Father Carl walked about the giant open room filled with rows of bunk beds, attempting to break into the souls of the dejected men and offer them solace. Pier Giorgio watched intently but spoke little.

On the way home, they stopped at a café and sat on the patio huddled around a small iron table draped with a tablecloth, enjoying a cup of coffee amidst the pleasant summer air which had cooled with the arrival of night.

"What of it, Georgie?" Father Carl suddenly said.

"I'm sorry?"

"You've not spoken ten words since we left Tobias's house."

"Have I not?"

"No. What's the matter?"

Pier Giorgio nodded.

"Well?"

After a pause, Pier Giorgio said, "I suppose I've stumbled onto an insight in noting the unusual circumstance we found ourselves in tonight."

"With the girl from the alley?"

"Yes. You see, I wondered if others would look in judgment and condemnation at the sight of you, a man of the cloth, carrying a girl plagued by vulnerability and presumably half your age, through the streets at such a late hour."

"Why would anyone look down upon us helping her?"

"They obviously should not, but I assure you in my native land of *Italia* the whispers of wrongdoing would persist for weeks. Many would have cried 'scandal' at the sight of a priest escorting a young girl home in such a condition. It's simply the way of things."

Father Carl pursed his lips and nodded in thought.

Pier Giorgio continued, "But here, it didn't seem to be an issue. This caused me to realize all the many ways I've witnessed you intertwine yourself with the community here, to the point that you're nearly a member of dozens, if not hundreds, of different families. You are entrenched in the community, like the keystone among the other stones. This is not the way of things in *Italia*. Priests are expected to be present on Sundays, at weddings and funerals, and perhaps occasionally for the confessional, but he is to be a phantom in the daily life of Italians. That is not to say they do not *try* to intercede into the comings and goings of their community, but it's with much effort and little success that they are able to accomplish all that I have seen you accomplish these last few months."

Pier Giorgio paused but sought more words; Father Carl could see it written on his troubled expression.

"Speak what's on your mind, Georgie. You sit with a friend."

Pier Giorgio flashed an appreciative but short smile and said, "I believe you know I've considered the priesthood. I've prayed for many years for an answer to what God wants me to do. Often prayers are answered in many forms, and I wonder if tonight that unfortunate girl was placed before us for a reason. I know that my family will not live in Germany forever, and I fear that if I return to Italy I will not be able to accomplish all I desire behind the white collar of the priesthood. In the lay state I will have better opportunities for daily contacts with the people, and so I can better help my brethren. It's not that I lack respect for Italian priests—far from it—I simply wish to be more involved with the poor and sick of my community and don't want to be held back by the constraints and demands of the clergy. Are such feelings an offense to God?"

Father Carl took a sip of his coffee before answering.

"I've known you a short while, Georgie, but I feel certain your offenses to God are few. The priesthood is not for everyone. God places a call in some men's hearts and not in others, but this does make the others worse men. And you, with your flame for charity and kindness, are probably better than most priests."

"This could never be true, Father."

"Oh, stop with your humility, boy. A light shines within you; I can see it as clear as the sunrise each morning. God has a plan for you, and if this plan steers you not toward the life I chose, then so be it. We may struggle to put into words the feeling of God calling us this way or that, but we can't deny those feelings are there, even if we can't make sense of them. Do not delay in the charitable missions you wish to pursue because you wrestle with guilt and agonize over this decision. Choose your path and commit to what's written in your heart."

Father Carl rose from the table, but Pier Giorgio remained seated.

"Now, I must return home and sleep, as I am quickly becoming an old man. But I leave you with my thanks for your assistance tonight, as well as this most humble bill, which I know you will gladly take care of for a poor man of the cloth."

Pier Giorgio smiled but could not find the words to match his wit, and so he sat in silence as Father Carl took his leave.

In October of that year Pier Giorgio traveled to Freiburg im Breisgdu, a city tucked in the southwest corner of Germany straddling the Dreisam River. It was at Father Carl's prompting that he took the train ride across Germany to live with the Rahner family for a period of a month. Pier Giorgio sought the tutelage of Father Carl's friend, Professor Rahner, the father of seven children and an acclaimed teacher of the German language, among other subjects that interested the young Italian.

For a month he immersed himself in the teachings of

Professor Rahner, hoping that by gaining a better understanding of the Germans and their language and culture, he could further help them in their struggle to move past the war and its aftereffects. He wanted especially to be able to relate to the young people, and so he found it necessary to learn from a teacher who had taught so many German students.

While there, however, he could not resist taking to the nearby Black Forest for hikes. The wooded hills, teeming abundantly with pines, firs, and birch trees, grew forth from the rumbling terrain of southwest Germany and boarded the view from Pier Giorgio's bedroom window. He disappeared for hours into the woods, lost in thought and prayer. Often, he would journey to the summit of Kandel, one of the highest peaks within the forest. Though it was not the rugged Alps of his homeland he cherished so much to climb, he took great pleasure in the seclusion and mystery of the Black Forest, pondering the advice Father Carl had given him about the priesthood and his calling to it; or rather, his lack thereof.

The issue began to crystallize within his soul and he came to terms with the fact that perhaps God had other plans for him outside the clergy. He *did* believe he could accomplish more as a layman and had always known this to be truth, but Father Carl had helped him accept this without the weight of guilt to accompany it.

In addition to this acceptance, Pier Giorgio enjoyed his time spent with the Rahner family, whose house was always bustling with the chaotic charm and undeniable love of a large family. Visions of his own children romping about the house and hiking through the surrounding countryside of a pleasant villa came to him in the form of sanguine daydreams. These desires, along with a good Catholic woman to share in the journey of parenthood, challenged further his aspirations of a priestly calling.

And so, during these peaceful days spent within the unfamiliar but comfortable confines of Germany's borders, Pier Giorgio's thoughts of the priesthood began to evaporate from the inner springs of his soul. Yet still, a Christian happiness welled within him and he took pleasure in pondering a future free from the weight of such a monumental decision.

"What now, does my future hold?" he whispered to himself, gazing out over the Black Forest from the summit of Kandel.

Grounded clouds trespassed upon the earth in the form of a morning fog, pervading the brush below and shrouding the trees. The fog complimented the view with a sense of mystery; a poetic symbol, he thought, to the unknown future awaiting him.

19

Combating the Black Shirts

The final days of October, 1922 changed the fate of all Italians when the Fascists, led by Benito Mussolini, seized control of the government during their March on Rome. The reaction to this dramatic upheaval within their country varied among the people, from enthusiastic support, to indifference, to enraged defiance. There was one young man who considered himself a part of the latter, and his rising voice in the back of the train cart was becoming hard for the other passengers to ignore. Their heads turned and glanced at him.

"These Fascists will destroy what we all cherish about our country," Pier Giorgio lamented to his friends. He didn't realize the vigor with which he was speaking. "I will remember this day for the rest of my life. Mussolini and his cronies have marched upon Rome and seized control; do you not realize this, friends? Have you not heard the news?"

"Yes, Georgie," his friend Antonio said, "how could we not know what has happened in Rome today, considering you spoke about it all throughout dinner? And now you continue to bore us with the topic on what would otherwise be a pleasant train ride to Santhia."

Others in the train cart laughed. Pier Giorgio was frustrated by their disinterest in the topic.

"You must calm down," another friend spoke up, "the Fascists will not be here for long. They're merely a broom we can make use of to sweep the Communists away."

"I must disagree," Pier Giorgio quickly replied. "I don't think each of you understands the gravity of what has happened with these 'Black Shirts' coming to power. Our country has had many issues since the end of the war—strikes and demonstrations, social injustice, even violence in the streets—but we must not cave in and give power to the first tyrant who comes along. Why will Mussolini be any better than the Communists who've caused so many problems for *Italia* in the last years?"

"You cannot deny that order seems to have been restored," a girl named Gia turned from her seat and said. "Do you not give Mussolini credit for this?"

"The Fascists have used violent tactics to put down the Bolsheviks; therefore, he has restored order through the very means he was attempting to rid our streets of. And let us not forget that the Black Shirts' aggression has been extended to many Catholic groups as well. I say again, none of you understand the sense of fear we should all have. Christianity, a religion of love, cannot come to terms with Fascism, a doctrine that exalts force and violence."

For some time, in the presence of his friends, Pier Giorgio continued to illustrate his discontent over the developments that had come out of Rome. It seemed his future, of which he had looked towards with hope and wonder just days prior in the forests of Germany, would now be complicated by the ominous cloud of Fascism.

Living mostly in Germany over the last year, he had not seen firsthand the increased presence of Mussolini's party throughout the streets of his homeland. He had heard rumors and stories, many passed along from his father, who received daily reports from his advisors on the changing political atmosphere in Italy. But Pier Giorgio never imagined it would come to this; that Benito Mussolini would soon become one of the most powerful men in all of Europe.

The Fascists had taken advantage of the chaos in Italy, where Communist and Catholic labor unions, farmers and industrialists, and upper and lower class citizens all opposed one another. They seized control with the stealth of a thief in the night, convincing all parties involved that they were a compromised answer. But Pier Giorgio felt adamantly otherwise, arguing that the Fascists were just as much a threat to the Church as the Communists.

Alfredo Frassati, while not caring much for the wellbeing of the Church, agreed with his son's fears concerning Mussolini and his followers.

"The rising of this man and his followers will do our country no good," he said over dinner one night. "I don't think I shall be Ambassador much longer if he comes to power."

His words were prophetic, as just weeks later the family was moving back to Turin after Alfredo turned in his resignation. The turnover in the Italian government led him back to his position at *La Stampa*, and so sadly for Pier

Giorgio, he was forced to leave Germany, a country he had grown to love.

"Mark my words," Pier Giorgio went on, steadying his body in the aisle as the train jostled along the tracks, "a day will come, I'm not sure how soon, but it will come, when you think back to my warning. You will not like what the Fascists bring to the front stoop of your home."

Just then, two men entered the last car and walked straight down the aisle to the group of young people. Pier Giorgio stood with his back to them, but turned about when his friends motioned with their heads of the new presence behind him. The men were dressed similarly, in black suits, and even looked the same, with square jaws and slicked-back hair.

"Friends," one of them said, "we are journeying about the train asking for donations to support the Fascist party and our new leader, Benito Mussolini. Though we have had great success in recent weeks, we still need your support. Won't you donate to the cause?"

He held out a bag toward Pier Giorgio in which to drop money in. The train remained silent, but a clutching pressure built within the tiny cart like a geyser on the verge of blowing, felt plainly by them all. Finally, after what felt like an hour but was no more than a few seconds, a burst of laughter erupted from Pier Giorgio's friends like a sudden clap of thunder.

"Yes," Antonio said composing himself, "I believe my friend here is a big supporter of your Cause, aren't you, Pier Giorgio?"

Others slapped him on the back, coxing him to donate.

The two men smiled, blissfully unaware of the joke. They continued to hold out their bags toward a stoic Pier Giorgio.

"I will not donate one lira to the likes of you," he said firmly. "I suggest you move to the next car."

Their expressions fell and they slid by Pier Giorgio, moving down the aisle. But before exiting the cart, one of them muttered, "You may not give now, but you will give later."

Over the succeeding months, Pier Giorgio bounced from one religious demonstration to the next, supporting the Church and doing his best to rally young people to combat the growing power of the Fascists. He organized prayers in the streets and served as bodyguards for priests, who were routinely becoming targets of the Black Shirts.

One winter day, amidst a brisk wind, he marched through the streets with his fellow members of the Cesare Balbo. They prayed aloud and sang hymns, holding the flag of their University's Catholic Club and marching peacefully toward the Cathedral for a Mass that was to be celebrated in their honor. But in the midst of the procession, Pier Giorgio spotted in the distance two rows of royal guards, the urban foot soldiers of Mussolini, wielding muskets and waiting to disperse the assembled crowd.

His friend, Marco Beltrano, grabbed his arm. "Georgie, do you see?"

"Of course I do. Keep marching and don't interrupt the Lord's Prayer."

"But what are we to do? They have rifles with them."

"I just told you what to do; keep marching and speak the Lord's Prayer beside your brethren."

Marco did as he was told, but the group of young men began to slow in their march. A few peeled off into a nearby alley and others meandered over to the sidewalk with their hands in their pockets, attempting to pass as innocent bystanders. Pier Giorgio remained at the head of the procession, holding tight to the Cesare Balbo flag.

Once upon the guards, dressed in full uniform and blue hats upon their heads, the procession stopped. One of the guards held up his hand. He was the largest of them all, a brute with massive arms bursting beneath the sleeves of his uniform and a full-grown beard layering his face. His voice was so deep it seemed to shake the ground when he spoke.

"This crowd must leave at once."

"Upon whose orders?" Pier Giorgio asked.

"This is none of your concern. You know who we are. You know the power we possess. This demonstration of Papists is over."

"You possess no power over our right to walk peacefully through the street," Pier Giorgio replied. "Now move at once, we must go meet our Lord in the Blessed Sacrament."

He moved forward along with a few other brave souls who followed his lead. But the guards braced themselves and blocked the way, crossing their muskets over one another to create barriers.

Pier Giorgio stepped back. He closed his eyes and prayed for patience.

"Gentlemen, what is it that you each have against me and my brothers? And do not reply with the doctrine that has been forcefully planted in your mind. Search your hearts, and tell us what it is that distresses you about us praying to our Lord."

Several of them glanced at one another, but only the lead guard spoke up.

"You Catholics cannot be trusted. You care more for your Church, your God, and your Virgin than you do for *Italia*. Your allegiances are a threat to the well-being of our country, and you must be put down. This is your last warning."

"My friend," Pier Giorgio said, "you have spoken foolishly, if I may be blunt. No man standing here today loves *Italia* more than I. But there is no reason I cannot have my Faith and my country."

"Did you call me a fool?" the man barked. He took a step forward and braced his rifle.

"No, listen, if I may explain in a gentler manner . . ."

The man grabbed at the flag in Pier Giorgio's hand and pushed him back, but Pier Giorgio held firmly to the wooden pole and they toppled over one another.

A scuffle ensued, with punches, shouts, and screams filling the street. Several guards fired shots into the air in an attempt to regain control, but it only spread more bedlam.

Some of Pier Giorgio's friends ran, while others stayed and fought. Below it all the lead guard and Pier Giorgio wrestled on the concrete, trying with all their might to rip the flag away from the other. It was as if the flag was a magical weapon that would determine the outcome of the brawl.

In the midst of the chaos, Pier Giorgio scolded his pride and his rage, the two dark twins churning beneath the surface of all men, for letting things come to this. Yet still, he could not let go of the flag.

Hours later, Pier Giorgio and four of his compatriots sat alongside one another on a tiny bench in the prison. They leaned up against the cement wall, sitting in the damp and dark cell. Behind the nearby toilet where a foul stench festered, a rat scurried about in search of scraps of food. Each of their heads ached and their bodies were covered with bruises and scars.

"I cannot believe this has happened," Marco moaned. "My parents are going to kill me."

Pier Giorgio put his arm around him. "I'm sorry, Marco, this is my fault. I let things escalate when this could've been avoided. But we must not paint ourselves as totally irrational men. What we did today was important."

"Why was it important? What difference could we have possibly made in standing up to them?"

"I cannot say for sure that we made a difference in the grand struggles we face today as young Catholics, but the difference is evident in our own souls. You see, we are men of faith, and therefore love and peace, but love and peace can only flourish when the Faith is not threatened. If you fight for goodness you may not always achieve your goals, but to simply partake in the fight makes the ultimate difference within us, for it gives us strength and we find our purpose in God. Rest assured, Marco, that to live without a Faith, without a patrimony to defend, without a steady struggle for the truth, is not living, but simply existing."

A guard came to the cell door.

"Frassati, you're free to go."

He stood up. "And what of my friends?"

"They might leave eventually, but your family name has done you a favor today; I don't think they knew who you were when they stopped you in the streets. Your grandmother is here to claim you."

Pier Giorgio sat back down, nudging himself between his friends. "I leave when they leave. Tell Grandmother Ametis she may return to my parent's home. She is a humble and selfless woman; she will understand if I do not come to meet her. But do give her a kiss upon her wrinkly cheek for me, won't you, Signor?"

His friends chuckled under their breath as the guard huffed and walked away. Several hours later, Pier Giorgio walked out of prison alongside his friends.

20

Comforting the Sick

The sunlight blanketed the square of Crocetta, save for the shade of the trees on the perimeter. Pier Giorgio held his rosary in one hand, while in the other he fooled with tiny pebbles he had scooped up off the ground. He sat with his back to the fountain in the center of the square. The water sprinkled up from a statue and returned to the pool below in soft splashes. A mist hung over the fountain and cooled him through his clothes. Such moments seeped in leisure, though few and far between, helped him forget about the political chaos of his country.

Through the trees and a sea of people gathering for picnics and recreation, he spotted his friend, Teresa Vigna. She was nearly twenty years his senior, and yet their rapport was that of equals. He waved and went to greet her with a hug.

"Teresa, it's good to see you!"

"And you, Georgie! These visits to the clinic possess much more cheer with you alongside me."

"How nice of you to say. I enjoy visiting your sick patients."

"The feeling is mutual from them. Each time you're unable to come with me, they ask of your whereabouts."

"Oh, no!" he exclaimed laughing. "Don't tell me this. Now, I must come with you *every* Saturday."

"Perhaps that was my aim. What's in the bag?" she asked, motioning toward the black bag resting at his feet.

He smiled and winked. "My bag of Catholic goodies."

Together they set out from the square and navigated their way through the busy streets of Turin. It seemed as if on this, the first day of warmth after a lingering winter, the city's inhabitants had come out of hibernation. The elderly sat outside their homes, children laughed and played in the street, and young lovers sat cuddling on park benches. Pier Giorgio never took conscious note of the malaise that set in during winter until the arrival of such spring days as this.

Nearly an hour later, the two of them walked into one of Turin's health clinics for the underprivileged. The smell inside was one of medication and chemicals mixed with human sickness, and the air was thick and muggy with the poor ventilation of the infirmary. They checked in at the front desk as volunteers and went to the back room where dozens of patients rested in beds, each with varying diseases and ailments. They were set up in rows, not five feet apart from one another. Coughs and moans echoed throughout the giant, hollow room.

Teresa and Pier Giorgio set off at once to the first row of beds. For each patient not resting in slumber, they crouched by the bedside. Teresa attended to a litany of their medical needs, while Pier Giorgio offered a smile and kind word. More often than not, a common reply came from every man, woman, and child.

"Pier Giorgio! You've returned to see me!"

He somehow assured them all with the utmost sincerity, rather than false flattery, that he'd come specifically to see them. From his bag of "goodies" he pulled rosaries, prayer cards, small crucifixes, and devotional books, distributing them among the sickly with spiritual advice on the importance of each item. To a small child he handed a book about the life of St. Catherine of Siena.

"Little one, this special woman spoke to Jesus during her earthly life. Perhaps you will too if you read about her."

For some it was the first gift they'd ever received, at least since the last time Pier Giorgio had come to visit.

After hours in the clinic, Teresa and Pier Giorgio said their goodbyes to the patients. Teresa stayed behind for a moment to fill out paperwork. When she emerged back outside, she saw Pier Giorgio sitting across the street, resting at the base of a tree and scribbling inside a leather journal. She waited for the cars to pass and crossed over.

"What are you doing?" she asked upon reaching him.

"Just going over my list of debts."

"I'm sorry?"

He put the journal back in his bag and stood up. "There are some kind men and women I owe."

"Owe what? Money?"

He chuckled. "Yes, of course."

"What do you owe them for?"

"I had to borrow from them to purchase all that came with us in this bag. Teresa, dear friend, do you think religious articles and books simply sprout forth from the earth like crops?"

"No, I just, I suppose I assumed with your family's

money . . ." Her words trailed off, lost in the haze of her befuddlement.

"No, no, my parents' money is not mine to distribute as I please. I have borrowed from others and will work to pay it back, although my Papa would probably rather I steal from him than go about town collecting debt. He finds my begging for money embarrassing to our family name."

"But does he know what you are collecting the money for?"

Pier Giorgio considered his answer before responding. "I think not. Shall we walk back across town?"

She smiled and together they headed back from the direction in which they had come. Once halfway, Teresa said, "You know, Georgie, you're a natural with those patients."

"Oh, I don't know. I cannot deliver them medical care as you can. You're a dream come to life for a clinic like that—a volunteer with actual medical expertise. I'm just a buffoon trying to make them laugh and smile."

"Do not undervalue the humor and compassion you show them, Georgie." After passing another block, Teresa said, "If you enjoy this work so much, you should come with me to visit the lepers at Saint-Lazare Hospital."

He stopped and grabbed her arm. "You're able to work with these people?"

"Yes, why are you so shocked?"

"I've tried in vain to reach them, but the strict rules concerning their isolation has kept me from them. Could you take me there now?"

"Now?"

"Yes, we must go at once. With you, I'll be able to get in, no?"

"Well, yes, I have permission, but I wasn't planning on going—"

Pier Giorgio cut her off, grabbing her arm and leading her down the road in a near sprint. He knew the way from all the previous times he'd tried to visit. Several times Teresa tried to persuade him to try another day, but her words repelled from his ears.

In the late afternoon, they moved through the front doors of Saint-Lazare Hospital, a clinic specifically for those plagued with leprosy. The lights in the main office were mostly burnt out, and the ones still on flickered with fading life. A woman waited at the front desk, but Pier Giorgio couldn't make out her features because they hid behind a mask. Her entire body was covered in a medical gown, with latex gloves gripped tightly to her hands as she handed the two of them a clipboard and form to fill out. She was perturbed by their lack of an appointment, but was familiar with Teresa and so looked past her regulations.

They were told to put on a protective gown similar to the one the woman behind the counter wore, including the gloves and mask. After putting it all on, they set out to another floor by way of a dingy, cement staircase.

It was a large building, with several stories and narrow corridors that stretched nearly an entire city block. But it was completely abandoned and possessed a gripping silence that hung heavily throughout the halls.

In a strange way the silence was deafening, a burden upon the ears, though in an inexplicable way. Pier Giorgio did not see another employee of the hospital, nor a patient, until Teresa led him into a corner room on the third floor.

Once inside they saw a nurse, also in full-body medical gear, attending to a young man as she dabbed his face with cotton swabs dipped in ointment. She stood over his bed in front of a row of windows flooded by sunlight, but peeked over her shoulder when they entered. Upon seeing Teresa, her eyes narrowed at their ends in response to the smile behind her mask. She nodded and went back to her work, unfazed by their sudden presence as the woman at the front desk had been.

On the opposite side of the room sat a couple, presumably married from the nearness of their positions on the floor and the demeanor in which they behaved, playing a card game with a girl no older than ten. Their heads also rose when Teresa and Pier Giorgio entered the room.

"Teresa, what a pleasant surprise," the woman said, smiling.

Unlike the employees and volunteers of the hospital, they were dressed in pajama-like attire, with matching blue robes, white-striped gowns, and no mask or gloves. Their faces bore the scars of their disease, scars as deep as ravines and as red as fire. Between the deep scars were rows of lumps and boils protruding from the skin, as if on the verge of popping through.

Teresa walked around the couch separating them. Pier Giorgio followed. They both took a seat on the couch.

"Yes," Teresa said, "I wasn't planning to come today, but this is my friend, Pier Giorgio; he wanted to come visit."

"Hello," Pier Giorgio greeted them with a smile.

"Good afternoon," the man said. His words were muffled by the skin peeling off his lips. "I'm Alberto Barnetti and this is my wife, Natalia. My daughter, Regina," he said motioning toward the young girl, "and my son over there is Anthony."

"What a wonderful family you're blessed with," Pier Giorgio replied. He looked down to the girl. Her innocent youth was tarnished by the white boils and craters growing across her face. Pier Giorgio's eyes began to water, but he composed himself and said, "What game are you playing, little one?"

"Scopa," she answered, shyly.

"Ah, a wonderful game. I often played this with my parents, just as you're doing now, but I've not played in many years; maybe soon you will play with me?"

She looked to her mother, who nodded.

"Okay, yes."

"Excellent!" he exclaimed.

A smile broke through her scars and boils.

"Pier Giorgio," the father said, "you seem like a good, young man; won't you go over and talk with my son? We've been in this hospital for almost a year and I know he yearns for another youth to give him company."

"Of course," Pier Giorgio said rising from the couch. He walked across the room, leaving Teresa to visit with the rest of the family, and waited for the nurse to finish caring for the boy. She wrapped most of his face in bandages, save for his eyes and lips. When she left, Pier Giorgio grabbed a stool and slid it by the bedside.

"Your father tells me your name is Anthony."

"Yes, who are you?"

His body nor his head rose from the bed and pillow, but his eyes focused in on Pier Giorgio.

"My name is Pier Giorgio Frassati."

"You've never been here before with Teresa."

"I didn't know she came here. I've tried before to visit, but was unable to. I am blessed to accompany her today."

Pier Giorgio suddenly felt uncomfortable with the mask gripping his face. He glanced over at the nurse making her way out of the room and pulled it down when she fell from sight around the wall. Anthony smiled.

"This is a nice room," Pier Giorgio said, "does your whole family live here?"

"Yes, we were all infected last spring. We've been here for a year but it's not so bad; it's bigger than our old home, and we have more furniture now."

"I admire your optimistic spirit, Anthony. I wish more of my friends were like you. Are there many patients here? I didn't see much activity in the halls—few doctors and nurses, other patients, visitors—where are they all?"

"I believe there are only a few dozen of us here in the hospital—patients, I mean. I suppose that's a good thing, that not many people from the outside are being infected. They keep us on separate floors and we each have only one nurse. Ours is Maria; she just left. There is only one doctor for the whole building. Not many people leap at the opportunity to work here, nor visit, for that matter. None of us have visitors, except for the occasional volunteer, like Teresa. She is wonderful to come. I once had many friends, but they're afraid to come visit me."

"That's unfortunate, but you're blessed to have your family, no? Your sister is quite the heart-breaker, very cute, that one is."

"Yes, I think my father is not so sad that she is confined to this hospital, for the boys might be knocking down our door if not."

"My father has that very problem with my sister," Pier Giorgio agreed, smiling.

"What's the weather like today?" Anthony asked.

Pier Giorgio hesitated. He glanced at the sunlight coming through the windows.

"You don't have to lie and tell me it's dreary," Anthony added. "I can enjoy it through your description."

Pier Giorgio nodded and smiled. "It's a glorious spring day, one of the first after a cold winter. The sunlight is a stranger to any cloud cover, but there's still a cool chill that masks the heat. I must tell you, Anthony, it's one of those days where every pretty girl in *Italia* realizes she has been hiding all winter and so they emerge all at once and overload your senses."

Anthony chuckled. "Do you play any sports, Pier Giorgio?"

"Yes, I like to swim, ski, and ride horses, and I was once quite good at fútball. But my main passion is for mountain climbing."

"Mountain climbing? How wonderful!"

"Yes, with every passing day, I fall madly in love with the mountains; their fascination attracts me. My climbs have a strange magic in them, so that no matter how many times they're repeated, and however alike they may be, they're never boring, in the same way as the experience of spring is never boring but fills our spirit with gladness and delight."

"Oh, how I'd love to climb into the clouds. I cannot think of a more enjoyable activity after sitting in bed for so many days."

"Perhaps you can come with me one day soon."

"No, we're not allowed to leave."

"I could sneak you out."

Anthony smiled. "I would not be able to get far. The leprosy has claimed one of my feet."

"Oh. I'm so sorry. I didn't know."

"How could you? I'm buried beneath these covers." After a pause, Anthony said, "But perhaps you could tell me of a recent climb you had. I'd enjoy hearing of it."

"Oh course!"

And so Pier Giorgio obliged, diving into a tale of his latest adventures in the mountains. He relayed a story of scaling Mount Mucrone, navigating his way through the fog and to the top where he attended Mass and received the Eucharist at a small chapel. When he came back out, the fog had cleared and he soaked in the panoramic view of the jagged and rolling mountains. Anthony lived it all from his bed, forgetting momentarily that his body was assailed by leprosy.

An hour later, Pier Giorgio and Teresa took their leave, assuring the Barnetti family that they would soon return. Outside, Pier Giorgio smiled and took a deep breath before they made their way back.

"That Anthony," he said, "what an amazing spirit. He

seems to possess no bitterness. His eyes were filled with life. Have you noticed?"

"Yes," Teresa answered. "He gets it from his parents."

"They are most gracious people. But what wealth we have, Teresa, to be in good health as we are."

She nodded and for three blocks they walked in silence, both knowing the other's thoughts still remained with the Barnetti family.

"I was thinking," Pier Giorgio said, "Anthony's deformation and that of his family's will disappear when they enter Paradise. But we have the duty of putting our health at the service of those who do not have it. To act otherwise would be to betray the gift of God. No human being should ever be left abandoned. The best of all charities is that consecrated to the sick. It's exceptional work, and you should be proud you've answered such a call, Teresa. Few have the courage to face its difficulties and dangers, to take on themselves the sufferings of others, in addition to their own needs, preoccupations, and cares."

"Thank you for your kind words, Georgie, but you too have answered such a call. I'm glad you came with me today."

They paused at the corner of a block where Teresa would wait for the bus to take her home.

"I couldn't have had the privilege of meeting such special souls without you. Thank you, Teresa."

Teresa smiled and hugged him. Before going their separate ways, they made plans to meet again in a week to visit the Barnetti family.

21
Atoning for Sins

Pier Giorgio gathered his supplies and packed them into his rucksack. He didn't want his mother to see his rope and other climbing tools for fear that she would worry about him journeying into the mountains, as she so often did. He opened his bedroom window and dropped them down to the ground some twenty feet below. They landed with a thud.

He left his room and arrived at the staircase just as his sister did. Her dark hair flowed elegantly atop her shoulders, as if she had spent the whole day perfecting it. She wore her favorite red dress and layers of make-up caked her face.

"My, you look beautiful, Luciana!"

"Thank you," she said, twirling around so that her dress fluttered in the air. When she stopped, she frowned. "You aren't dressed for the Shrove Carnival. You look like you're dressed for a climb."

"You know me well," he replied, wondering if his mother would be as observant as she had been.

"Georgie! Why are you not coming to meet everyone and have fun? The Carnival does not happen every other week."

"And that's a good thing," he said as he began to descend the stairs.

"What is that supposed to mean?" she asked, following after him.

"There is much sin and debauchery amidst the *fun* of the Carnival. You would be wise to come with me instead."

"I've already made plans to meet my friends. But lighten up, brother; not everything in life has to be so dramatic."

He stopped at the bottom of the stairs and turned to face her. She was following so closely she nearly bumped into him from the last stair.

"I feel that few people would accuse me of being 'dramatic,' or that I would not know how to enjoy myself; but nothing, in my view, is more dramatic than our sins. Those streets out there are filled with those who care little for matters of the soul. All they concern themselves with are pleasures of the flesh. The season of lent is almost upon us; we should be focusing on prayer and fasting, not dance and drinking." When she didn't respond, he went on. "And while we're on the topic of my lecturing you, why did you abandon Natalia on the slopes last weekend?"

"What?"

"I saw you leave that poor girl behind to go off with your other friends."

"Because she kept falling down. How could I go ski with everyone else if I was constantly stopping to help her up and show her how to stay on her feet for more than ten seconds?"

"Her feelings are far more important than your contentment. You know she's a clumsy girl and cannot help it."

"I'm sure you helped her, so I have nothing to worry about." He opened his mouth for a rebuttal but ate his words and paused. "You did, didn't you? You went over and helped her ski the rest of the day."

"That's not important."

"My," she chuckled sarcastically, "being your sister has its challenges."

He smiled and grabbed her shoulders, which were level with his since she stood on the step. "I don't mean to pester you, Luciana, but I'm your big brother; if I don't keep you in line, who will? Just promise me you'll be careful this weekend."

"Of course I will."

"And you will not miss Mass on Sunday?" he asked with a raise of his brow.

"How long will you be in the mountains?"

"All weekend. Do not change the subject—will you be at Mass this weekend? I know you missed two Sundays ago."

"How did you . . ." she nodded her head. "Yes, I'll go."

"Good. Now where are Mama and Papa?"

"They went out to dinner with friends."

She moved by him and headed for the door, blowing him a kiss before leaving the house.Pier Giorgio sighed. He had not seen either of his parents in two days with their conflicting schedules. He had hoped to see them before his weekend trip. But his spirits lifted when he heard his grandmother shuffling into the nearby den with the aid of her cane.

"Grandmother Ametis, how I love when you come to

stay with us. It brings me such joy to just see you walk by." He followed her into the room and helped her sit down on the couch. "May I get you anything?"

"No, thank you, dear boy. Where are you going?" She lifted her tired feet up as Pier Giorgio draped a blanket over her.

"I'm going to adoration and then to spend the weekend climbing Mont Blanc."

"Good for you; at least someone in this family still prays."

"I believe there are others under this roof who pray," he replied, "at least when you come to visit."

She smiled. "And what will you be praying for tonight at adoration, Georgie?"

"As a member of the men's Catholic Club at the university, they've asked us all to pray for our fellow young people who are out tantalizing the streets at the Carnival."

"Ah, young people like your sister?"

"Yes, I've already warned her of the dangers of this week."

"You should warn your parents; I believe they'll be decorating the town with their presence as well. So many years they've done this. I remember your mother always returning in the early hours of morning as a young woman during the Shrove Carnival. Like you, I prayed fervently for her safety. I still do."

"We both will," he said leaning down to kiss her.

"I wish I could join you at adoration, but . . ." she pointed down to her legs.

"I understand, and so does the Lord. Do you have

someone to take you to Mass on Sunday?"

She thought for a moment. "Some weekends when you're gone, your mother or sister will take me, but I'm not sure they will with the Carnival going on. Sleep might be their closest companion come Sunday morning."

"Then I shall return early from my expedition and we'll go together. I need to make sure Luciana goes anyway."

"No, please don't. I can manage to get there somehow."

"Not another word, beautiful lady. I'll see you Sunday morning."

"Where are you going?"

Pier Giorgio hesitated, unsure of how to respond. Her eyes told him her latest question was genuine. She'd already forgotten.

"To adoration, and then the mountains."

"Good boy; at least someone in this family still prays."

Pier Giorgio nodded and leaned down to kiss her on the cheek, uttering a quick prayer for her fading mind before leaving her side.

Outside, the sounds of the bustling streets bounced overhead. Music blared and people playfully screamed and laughed. Pedestrians filed down the road in bunches before the Frassati house, hurrying off toward the activity of the Carnival with fears that they had already missed out on some of the excitement. He was amazed they could all focus on such a carefree life when the Fascists were still threatening the freedom of the Italian people.

After retrieving his rucksack from the side of the house, he moved across town toward the Cathedral's adoration chapel. He passed a different party, parade, and concert with each block, avoiding as best he could the drunkards stumbling about as they stammered loudly about inconsequential nonsense. He prayed for the patience to forego his judgment and frustration toward them.

Minutes later, he was kneeling before the Blessed Sacrament in a dark room lit up only by the votive candles bordering the walls. Silence descended upon him as the chaos of the outside streets dissipated into the night. He bowed his head, rosary in hand, and fell into a sea of prayer.

His eyes were closed, but beneath his eyelids he saw his prayers rising to God, as if clinging to the wings of butterflies drifting up in search of the gardens of heaven, gardens tended to by the seraphim as they pruned the prayers of the faithful. He asked for sanctity in which to bring others to Christ, and sought forgiveness for the sins of his brothers and sisters outside.

Pier Giorgio was in such a trance, he failed to notice the coming and going of the night.

* * * * *

Chaos danced through the streets of Turin, but chaos cloaked in this guise of fun. The Shrove Carnival came only once a year, preceding the religious season of lent. Somewhere along the line the city and its inhabitants had begun to focus solely on this massive street party instead of the time of fasting, prayer and almsgiving that was supposed to follow.

Alfredo and Adelaide had begun a tradition some years ago where they attended a wine tasting at a restaurant in the center of town. For several hours they stood on a second floor balcony overlooking the square, tasting all sorts of merlots and chardonnays as they gossiped with friends about all the menial comings and goings of life in Turin. After the tasting, they'd gravitate inside and eat the finest Italian food by candlelight. A common joke throughout the evening was that they and their friends were all too old to participate in the actual Carnival events, so they convened here to get away from it all.

Luciana, meanwhile, had never danced so much in all her life. She navigated her way through the streets from one party to the next as the music flowed through her veins. Deep into the night she drank wine, danced, sent flirtatious smiles toward handsome boys, and laughed with friends, letting go of the daily stresses of her life.

Pier Giorgio's friends—Marco, Camillo, Tonino, Guardia, and all the others—also made their way through the streets of Turin, hitting up all the hotspots of the Carnival. This was their favorite time of the year. Beautiful girls were everywhere, made even more beautiful by the mood of the evening. The boys joined in fellowship, wrapping their arms around one another and singing along to the bands whose music filled the air.

The city was alive and vibrant, with no plans to sleep tonight. Even the poorer districts were bustling with energy. Restaurants and bars were packed, the streets full, and lights glittered all about the streets, shining brighter than the stars hanging above.

Only one spot rested quietly in solitude.

* * * * *

Pier Giorgio opened his eyes and peered around the room. There had been several others with him earlier, but now he was alone. He noted the time on his watch and saw that wax had dripped from a nearby candle onto his fingers. He hadn't noticed.

Once outside, as he gazed upon the first glimmers of sunlight over the horizon, he was struck by how long he had actually been in adoration. He laughed to himself and walked over toward the Polytechnic campus. Before leaving town, he wanted to post some fliers about the upcoming meeting of the Cesare Balbo.

Pier Giorgio navigated his way to the center of campus in search of the boards where students posted news; three walls of cork mended together in the shape of a triangle. He tacked up his fliers, but upon turning around was met by two stumbling men laughing and singing. They noted his presence before he could sneak away.

"Ah! Hello there, b-b-boy!" one of them said.

Pier Giorgio smiled and nodded.

One took a swig from the bottle in his hand and passed it to the next. After he took a gulp he held it out to Pier Giorgio.

"No, thank you."

"Too good for our wine?"

"Of course not, but I'm not out for drinking tonight."

They laughed. "Who in his right mind would *not* be out for drinking tonight?"

"I suppose me," he answered calmly, attempting to walk by them.

"Well, what is it you're doing out so late, or . . . or *early*, I suppose we should say. What *is* the hour?" They laughed again as they stumbled over toward the posters Pier Giorgio had tacked up.

"Oh, look here," one of them said, "we have a good Catholic boy putting up fliers for his meeting, and in the dead of night on the week of the Carnival. How typical, no?"

"Typical, yes, absolutely, no surprise at all," the other one agreed, mumbling incessantly before taking another swig of wine.

Pier Giorgio turned about.

"What a way to ruin such fun," one of them said, staring at the fliers and squinting to see through his inebriation. "This cannot stay up. Leave your religious meetings for another week, b-b-boy!"

He reached up to rip the flier down, but not a second later, in movements so swift it seemed impossible, Pier Giorgio grabbed his wrist, gripped it tightly, and stared deep into his murky eyes.

"I recommend you don't do that," he commanded.

"And what if I do?"

His breath was soaked in stale alcohol.

"It's your choice on whether you wish to discover the answer to that."

Their eyes remained locked, only inches apart, until the other one said, "Come, Diego, let's leave this fool to his fliers and club meetings. We can't let him ruin our evening, or morning, . . . hah! What *is* the hour, anyway?"

They broke into laughter and disappeared into the shadows. Pier Giorgio took a deep breath and smoothed the edge of his flier back up on the board.

He caught a train west toward Mont Blanc, noting for the first time that he'd been awake all night, just as many of the Carnival-goers had been. Yet, he was not weary. He exited at the proper station and began his hike toward the mountain. The sun blazed with orange brilliance but was low enough in the sky that its rays withheld from burning one's eyes. In the low plateaus, he came across a pasture of tall grass where a flock of butterflies was gathered, resting peacefully on the tips of each blade. He smiled and took off in a sprint, running through them and dispersing the butterflies into the air. They floated up, their colorful wings flapping against the blue of the sky.

Upward he then climbed, continuing with his prayers. He pondered the puzzling wonder in which he could feel so close to God in the confines of a small, dark room, and yet feel just as close to him in the vast expanse of the Alps. It was the mystery of the Faith, in that he understood it on some subconscious level, and yet, he could not explain it.

In the course of the next twenty-four hours he refrained from eating anything, drinking only water to renew his strength. He wandered about the side of the mountain, finding pleasant areas in which to utter his prayers—in the limbs of a pine, beneath a cliff, atop a gorge, at the mouth of a cave. He pitched a tent and departed early for bed, bundling himself in blankets to shield the bitter cold.

The next day he awoke at dawn and descended the mountain, arriving home in time to take his grandmother to Mass. While he waited for her to get ready, he poked his head in Luciana's room, but her bed was empty.

The family's maid was walking the hallway.

"Mariscia, where is Luciana?"

"I believe she spent the night at a friend's house, Georgie," she replied. "You know how crazy things are at the Carnival. But I'm sure she's alright."

"Oh . . . alright, yes, thank you."

Pier Giorgio walked down to his parents' bedroom and cracked the door. Both of them were sleeping. He shut the door and went back downstairs. Grandmother Ametis was ready and waiting.

"Ready, Georgie?"

"Yes, of course."

He smiled and escorted her out through the front door.

22

The Shady Characters

Pier Giorgio was surprised when his eyes began to water. His emotions ran over him like a herd of beasts as Father Robotti lead him in his final promises, standing just before the altar at the Chapel at Our Lady of Grace in Turin's Church of San Domenico. But these were not the priestly vows he had pictured himself making one day, rather, he was being received into the Third Dominican Order, a lay group dedicated to a defense of the Faith and a devotion to ardent prayer life.

It was a commitment three years in the making, juggled between dozens of other duties he had undertaken, including his continued education at the Polytechnic. But the decision to join the Order was affirmed with confidence when he made the decision in Germany to forego a priestly calling.

He had always been enamored with Dominican spirituality and found this intimate group as a way to further his relationship with God. It was a sort of compromise, he thought, to becoming a man of the cloth.

In the months that followed he attacked his new role within the Order just as he had done with the St. Vincent de Paul Society, the Marian Sodality, the Apostleship of Prayer, and every other organization to which he held claim. Through so many of these groups he continued to combat Fascism, which was spreading like untamed vines of ivy across the churches of Italy and threatening the Faith with their vice-like grip on religious freedoms.

But amidst the struggles of his daily life, he found time for solace as well in the form of friendship. The bliss of common interests found in several other young people helped ease the worries of his hectic life; it was a common interest that, without surprise, involved his love for the mountains.

At the end of another long week of studies at the Polytechnic, he stopped by the Cathedral on his way home to pray for the safe travels of his forthcoming expedition. An hour later he frantically packed up his belongings and sprinted over to the train station. Gathered there together, loading their luggage below the train, was the group known as "The Shady Characters."

"Oh!" Marco exclaimed. "There's our final member, and a founding member at that. We were afraid we'd have to leave without you."

"I'm sorry for my tardiness," Pier Giorgio panted, throwing his things below the train.

"What were you doing?" asked his friend Isidoro.

"Must you even ask?" Marco interjected. "He was somewhere close to a tabernacle, no?"

Pier Giorgio answered by way of a silent smile and they all laughed. Inside the train, they took their seats and prepared for their journey west toward the French border, a journey that would ultimately lead them to a small hostel resting atop the Alps known as the Little St. Bernard.

In a series of events lost to a clouded memory, Pier Giorgio had helped found this casual but important club consisting of nearly a dozen young, Christian mountain climbers. Their unusual name derived from a desire to seem mysterious to outsiders, though in most regards the name was no more than a joke. Their comings and goings were never of the serious sort, and it was fairly common for all their energy to be devoted to pranks played on one another. But they came together in fellowship several times a month, usually culminating with a weekend mountain excursion.

The group consisted of men *and* women, which was unusual, as most groups separated the sexes. But this was what Pier Giorgio loved about the unofficial "Society." It was not regulated by the rules and regulations that so many organizations were confined by. It was a dynamic gathering of people, adding and losing members with each meeting, but Pier Giorgio remained ever at the center of them all, as if he were the timber that kept their fire roaring with life.

He glanced around the car, eyeing each of his friends sitting beneath the dim, flickering lights of the train. He watched, unbeknownst to them, as they laughed and told stories and discussed the impending weekend climb. Pier Giorgio knew these moments ran deeper than they appeared on the surface. While he viewed their camaraderie as a means of recreation and relaxation, he knew the time he spent with these friends was a way to lasso their souls toward Christ. Their guards were down on such occasions, their watchful dragons resting in jaded slumber. It was here, Pier Giorgio knew, that he could bring the Faith to them, perhaps without them even realizing it.

In many ways, it astounded Pier Giorgio that so many of his youthful brethren went about each day without a second thought to the world to come. He worried for them more than they could possibly fathom; he worried, in fact, for their own souls more than perhaps they did themselves. He was free of condemnation and judgment, for he was not without his own transgressions, and his friends were certainly not forged from the fires of great evil. But he noticed as the years passed that they were coasting through life, at first dipping their toes into the lakes of sin, but in time had stood back up and seemed to be bracing themselves for a plunge, headfirst, into such tainted waters.

Pier Giorgio prayed that they would stop, if but for a breath, to consider the capacity in which God viewed their sins, and in doing so they might combat the hypnotic trance of this world and its materialistic and self-gratifying demons. Such trips into the towering stratospheres of the Alps were a haven where Pier Giorgio knew he could reach them, and it was such trips that confirmed his decision to forego his inclination to the priesthood. As a layman, as a friend, he could reach them more intimately.

At the last stop, the group exited the train and retrieved their luggage. They quickly changed into their climbing gear so as to set out toward the hostel and reach it before nightfall. Pier Giorgio led the way through a hiking trail that sent them up toward the clouds, navigating their way through the pine forests and eventually scaling steep gorges and cliffs. They worked together and respected the mountains at moments of peril, moving slowly and linking themselves with rope, and at simpler moments they laughed and told stories, as if strolling through a park resting thousands of feet above sea level.

The Little St. Bernard, with its stone walls and tin roof, came into view just as the sun's rays disappeared beyond the surrounding cliffs. The group broke into cheers and sprinted across the flat terrain leading up the entrance.

After checking in, Pier Giorgio broke off from the group to check on the status of a visitor he'd asked to come without the knowledge of the rest of the group. He located the room given to Monsignor Pinardi and knocked on the door. The older priest, nearly bald and slightly overweight, came to greet him.

"I hope you are well, Monsignor. I cannot thank you enough for making the trip."

"Thank you for inviting me Georgie, and for picking up the cost on my room."

"Of course. It's a small cost in exchange for your celebrating Mass tomorrow. I will see you in the morning, then?"

"Yes, bright and early."

"Wonderful!"

Pier Giorgio departed down the hall and found his way to the servant quarters, greeting all the employees of the hostel—the cooks, maids, and custodians—with smiles and hugs. He inquired about their health and how their families were doing, and asked them to come to Mass in the morning.

He joined his friends in the dining hall and sat down to break bread with them. The fellowship of good conversation and company continued, with the added benefit of wine and pipes whose consumption had been delayed on the journey there. There were a few other patrons staying at the hostel, but none who possessed the energy of the Shady Characters and the ability to be the life of the party.

After dinner, they retreated to their rooms momentarily to bundle themselves in warmer clothing. A tradition awaited, that of a short hike to a nearby waterfall just beyond the hostel grounds, hidden a half-kilometer away behind a small cliff. The area was only reached with great care. Pier Giorgio and several of the men lit lanterns and led everyone else through the darkness of the alpine woods, around the cliff by means of a dirt trail and to a clearing just next to the waterfall. They built a campfire on the bank of the river and settled into a circle to prolong their evening.

"I wonder how many souls have frequented this spot before us," Giuseppe mused, "I cannot image it is many."

"No, not many at all," agreed Christina, a young brunette with sharp features and engaging eyes of hazel. "We've never seen any other guests of the Bernard here before. It's too hidden."

"Does this not make you stop to appreciate what we've found . . ." Giuseppe asked no one in particular, ". . . to think that we presently rest in a spot where perhaps only a few souls have come in the entire world's history?"

"We Shady Characters are first-class adventurers," Pier Giorgio said proudly, still working on his pipe from dinner. The fire in the center popped with life.

"Where did you sneak off to before dinner, Georgie?" asked Clementina, the unofficial leader of the Shady Characters.

"Ah, so you noticed? I went to see a surprise guest whom I have invited."

"Who?" Marco asked.

"Monsignor Pinardi has agreed to come say Mass for us first thing in the morning."

A few of them moaned playfully.

"Georgie," Isidoro broke in, "tomorrow is Saturday. We'll go to Mass on Sunday morning."

"There's no harm in going to Mass two days in a row," Pier Giorgio reasoned. "I have invited him all this way, so I will be in attendance. But anyone who wishes to make other plans may do so. I've spoken with many of the servants of the Bernard and they will be there."

After a short pause, a young man new to the group, Ernesto, said, "I feel no different when I have left Mass; it seems if I had not gone at all, nothing would be different."

"You must not say this," Pier Giorgio said, turning his focus toward the new member.

"I don't wish to feel this way. I have guilt over these feelings, but yet, it's the way I feel."

"I understand, Ernesto, I do. There is no denying that the human mind is weak and tempted to boredom by habitual practices like our sacred Mass. I've found myself pondering trivial matters while sitting in the pews, like my next exam at school, or how to get back at Marco for putting that rotten egg in my shoe the last time we came up here."

Everyone laughed.

"I'm ready for you," Marco said confidently.

"Yes, sleep with one eye open, my friend." Pier Giorgio chuckled and went on. "But Ernesto, I promise you, the unseen graces received from the Mass—from the Word and the Flesh you consume—is beyond measure. We all fight inner battles, do we not? Battles against sins we know are wrong; battles against the moments of our sadness or depression, or rage or temptation?"

He looked around the circle, but no one answered.

"How is it that we are able to fight these inner battles? By turning to drink? To dance? To sport? To climbing mountains like this? All these are only temporary solutions, if solutions at all. It is only by feeding on the Bread of Angels that we gain the strength to fight these battles against passion and all adversities, because Christ has promised eternal life and the graces necessary to obtain it to those who feed on the Holy Eucharist. And when you are totally consumed by this Eucharistic fire, then you will be able, more consciously, to thank God who has called you to become a part of that multitude, and you will enjoy the peace that those who are happy in accordance with this world have never experienced, because true happiness does not consist in the pleasures of this world or in earthly things, but in peace of conscience, which we only have if we are pure in heart and mind."

"Poor Ernesto," Isidoro said shaking his head, "he had no way of knowing he would set off our club's Minister of Christ."

Several of them laughed and attempted to change the

subject, but a young man named Bertone brought the topic back.

"I know the importance of Mass. But I do not see, Georgie, how you are able to keep such a strong faith. Does it not waver at times? It must, with all that's happening in *Italia* with the Fascists. Did you hear about the priest who was beaten to the point of near-death in Florence last week?"

Pier Giorgio nodded. "Yes, of course."

"I am angered that God would allow such a thing to happen," Bertone added.

"I'm angered by this as well, but we must not direct our anger at God. He did not commit these acts. Those men did, and we must pray for them just as much as we pray for the recovering priest, if not more. Remember that the men who performed this heinous act had the free will to forego their violent urges. Free will allows such things to happen, but God must give us this freedom, for only then can we truly choose to love him. But yes, Bertone, my faith wavers at times. How could it not with all the pain and sadness of this world? At times I feel like a man drowning, searching for the strength for one more stroke. But it's only through faith that we can find meaning in it all. Faith is the anchor of our salvation; therefore, we must cling to it tightly. It is the only thing which allows us to bear the thorns with which are lives are woven. What would our life be without it? Nothing, or rather it would be spent uselessly, because in the world there is much sorrow, and sorrow without faith is unbearable. But sorrow lit by the torch of faith becomes a beautiful thing because it tempers the soul to the struggle."

"Our faith can be strong," Christina said from across the flames of the fire, "but what will we do without our Church, Georgie, when it falls to the Fascists who wish to destroy it?"

"If our faith is strong our Church will be strong as well. The times we're going through are difficult, because cruel persecution of the Church is raging. But you bold, young people," he said peering around the circle, "you should not be afraid of this small thing known as Fascism. Do you not know that we win?" he asked laughing. "It has already been written; remember that the Church is a divine institution and cannot come to an end. She will last till the end of the world. Not even the gates of hell can prevail against her. So I say, bring it on Benito!"

He stood up and pounded his chest like a gorilla. They all laughed.

"You should be careful," Marco offered, "Mussolini is likely to have spies in these woods."

Pier Giorgio jumped behind a tree stump, poking his head up like a groundhog. Marco, filled with perhaps too much wine, jumped on top of him and the two wrestled amidst the laughter of the rest of the group.

Moments later, the commotion dissipated. Clementina threw another log on the fire and the group settled back in.

"Alright," Ernesto said, "I will come to Mass with you tomorrow. How could I not after such words you have graced us with?"

"Yes," Giuseppe agreed, "we'll all be there, in order to make our fearless leader happy."

"Wonderful!" Pier Giorgio exclaimed.

The conversation turned back to trivial matters, to which Pier Giorgio contributed little. He decided he had commanded enough of the conversation already. So he sat quietly in the glow of the fire, peeking at a member of the group who had remained silent throughout most of the trip. His eyes fought the temptation to glance at her every so often, but Laura Hidalgo was like an optical magnet to which he was powerless against.

23
The Haze of Love

He wrote her letters. Many of them. But, as a fool afraid to disclose what was blossoming within his heart, he hid his love from the one to which his feelings were directed to by writing letters to *all* the members of the Shady Characters.

The idea came to him in a panic after he had dropped off the first of his letters to Laura at the post office. He pictured her opening it, surprised to get something from him in the mail. She would no doubt ask Christina and some of the other members of their club if they too had received letters from Pier Giorgio. When they replied that they had not, her suspicion would set in and his feelings for her would become a common topic of conversation among the group. The horror was too ghastly to imagine.

He raced back home and scribbled almost a dozen more letters to the other Shady Characters, thanking them for their most recent trip into the mountains and ensuring he would pray for them all and their families. He dropped the additional letters in the mailbox and thus, his love for Laura was cloaked in the guise of a furious letter-writing campaign which would last for months. Each time he would write to Laura, he would write to them all. The time and hand cramps were worth the trouble when he considered how often he thought of her. He viewed the mundane correspondence as love letters, but had no idea how she viewed them.

He wrote to her in 1924 of a trip he took into the mountains without the rest of the club:

> Dearest Laura,
>
> To the most kind secretary of the Shady Characters as well as cook, a Grivoline bombardment!
> I spent the night at the shelter last week and on a marvelous Saturday morning I climbed to the top regretting the absence of all of you, not only for the pleasure of sharing the great joy of planting one's foot on the much-longed-for summit, but also for the delightful company. I also missed the good lunches and especially the sandwiches that you know how to make so well.
> I enclose a gentian for you that I picked near the Vittorio Sella shelter. My friend Abbot Henry says that "maidens are like flowers," and so I think that like things like each other.
> What nice things are you up to? Do write back soon.
>
> Cordial alpinist greetings from,
>
> Pier Giorgio

At times, Laura would send a return letter, but not always. Like most young men befuddled by the mysteries of the female gender, Pier Giorgio struggled to place her feelings toward him, and without the confidence of his love being returned whole-heartily, he continued to conceal his own emotions.

The source of his love for Laura stemmed from multiple avenues, the first of which was her palpable beauty. Her high cheek bones and piercing eyes drew him into a kind of trance each time he looked at her, and her tanned skin matched the rich beauty of her long, dark hair. Her figure was slender but athletic, which was evident when she failed to lag behind the men on their climbs. She seemed to always smell wonderful, like wildflowers, he thought, and she dressed as a woman who cared little for attention yet still received it.

But her appearance came secondary to the woman she was. It took several conversations with Laura, mostly on their trips into the mountains, for Pier Giorgio to discover that she was an orphan. Her parents had left her and her brother at a children's home outside Turin, but this moment was beyond the reach of her memory and so her parents were ghosts of a distant and foreign past.

There she lived with her brother and dozens of other castaways until the age of eighteen when she left for the city along with her brother. She obtained a job, secured an apartment, and had been caring for herself and her brother ever since. Pier Giorgio listened sympathetically as she told her story beneath a pine tree near the Little St. Bernard. But beyond the caring expression on his face hid a smile, not in a sense of wicked enjoyment at her sorrow; rather, because he knew even before learning her story that she would possess such a caring and powerful spirit. He saw it inside her as clear as day, a sort of diamond encrusted in her soul that shone forth with the light of the Holy Spirit, acting as the source of her corporal beauty. He admired the care she gave her brother and the lack of resentment which she held toward her parents.

Still, the fumbled and confused state of Pier Giorgio's psyche over Laura prolonged the roundabout courtship. He'd been on several dates before and had spent many of his formative years in the presence of young ladies, several of them quite stunning. But none had bewildered him this way. So he strolled rather circuitously through a haze of love for some time, lost in his path but intoxicated by the feeling. Eventually, he turned to the only source of aid he could think of.

Pier Giorgio walked across the hall from his bedroom and knocked on the door.

"Yes?" cried Luciana from the other side. Her voice was muffled behind the door.

"It's me. May I come in?"

"Just a minute." He waited patiently before she opened the door. "What is it? I'm getting dressed to go out." She stood holding a towel over her chest and her hair was wet from a recent shower.

"Oh, alright, I don't want to hold you."

Luciana could see something brewing beneath his dark eyes.

"What is it, Georgie? Tell me."

"I had a question, of sorts."

"Well . . ."

"It's not so simple."

She sighed. "Let me get dressed and you can walk me to the train."

"That would be wonderful! I'd enjoy some exercise anyway."

Pier Giorgio meandered downstairs, passing his mother on the way down. Her face was void of color and she moved slowly, each step a struggle.

"Mama, you don't look well. Are you alright?"

"Another one of my migraines," came her exhausted reply.

"So many you've had. Bless you, Mama. I'll escort you to bed."

He wrapped his arm around her and supported her up the rest of the stairs, down the hallway and into her bed.

"Where is Papa?" he asked after dabbing a cold cloth over her forehead. "Someone should watch after you, but Luciana and I are on the verge of a walk."

"I haven't a clue of your father's whereabouts, nor do I ever. Mariscia is downstairs; she will watch after me. You children take your walk."

"But she probably has much housework to do. Perhaps I'll stay."

"No, Georgie. Leave me be. I just want to be alone."

"Yes, Mama."

He kissed her on the cheek and left the room.

Outside on the front stoop, he waited for his sister. With his hands in his pockets he strolled back and forth a few feet at a time. He was worried for his mother, who had been ill in the last weeks, and was frustrated that his father was not around more to care for her. Yet, at the same time he appreciated the work his father was doing at *La Stampa* in speaking out against the Fascists. Each day he reported on stories across Italy of the Black Shirts abusing their new-found power through the use of violence and intimidation.

Luciana emerged from the house nestling a hat neatly down over her long hair, one that matched the forest green in her dress.

"Alright, brother, let's walk and talk."

They departed down the road and turned toward the train station. For several blocks Pier Giorgio spoke of the weather, his most recent trip to the shore, and his frustration that many of his Catholic brethren were making concessions with the Fascists. His sister saw directly through these stalling tactics.

"Georgie, out with it. You talk like this all the time; you would have no need to accompany me to the station to discuss these things. What is it you *really* wanted to talk about?"

He chuckled. "Yes, I suppose you're correct."

"Well?"

He watched the traffic buzz by as they waited to cross the intersection.

"You see, I had questions for you, about . . ."

"About what?"

". . . about a girl."

"What?" Her face suddenly radiated as she slapped his shoulder. "Who? Who is this girl?"

"Quiet down," he commanded. "All of Turin can hear you."

"Tell me," she whispered, giggling like a child.

"She's one of the Shady Characters."

"Oh." Her expression dropped. "Such a strange group you have there."

"We enjoy ourselves," he replied smiling. "But we are harmless."

The traffic stopped and they crossed the street.

"Well, who is she?"

"Laura. Laura Hidalgo." He said her name proudly, as if introducing her as his spouse.

Luciana searched her memory. "Have I met her?"

"I don't think so."

"Well, what do you want from me? Advice on how to win her heart? I'm surprised you would need such help from me; the girls have always been fond of you."

"That is far from the truth, but I suppose I do need advice. I'm not sure how to tell if her feelings for me are mutual. I've not told anyone else this, but I believe I love this girl, Luciana. It amazes me how much I think of her throughout the day. Each time I'm away from her and I see a sunset, I wish to tell her about it. How strange is that?"

"Not so strange, if you love her. I feel the same way about Jan."

"Ah, yes, you seem quite fond of this new boy you've begun to see."

"He is no 'boy!' He's a *man* of the highest esteem."

Pier Giorgio laughed. "I know what ruffles your feathers, sister."

"Yes, well, I'm on my way to see him now, but don't tell mother."

"Your secret is safe with me," he promised. After the passing of another block, he said, "Do you suppose mother and father once wished to tell each other about the sunsets they had seen?"

Luciana considered her response for some time. "I think there was a time they did."

"And now? Do you think they still would discuss the sunsets they'd seen?"

"I believe once you're wed you should be watching sunsets together, no?"

Pier Giorgio nodded. At the turning of the next corner, the train station came into view. "I'll let you be on your way," he said.

"But I didn't even help you."

"I don't know what I expected you to do for me, but it was nice to simply tell someone about my feelings. I feel as though a weight has been lifted from my shoulders."

"Perhaps you could invite her over and I could meet her. I could see the way she interacts toward you. I no doubt will be able to tell what she thinks of you; women can read other women like books."

"Yes! What a wonderful idea. But . . ."

"What is it?"

"It may seem strange for me to invite her to tea with us."

"Invite her friends as well. It will be like a party."

"Yes! My, you are surely the brilliant one in this family."

"That could be true," she agreed with a shrug.

"Hah! You see, I knew I was right to tell you. I'll go home now and organize the gathering."

Pier Giorgio hugged her, leaving her at the entrance to the train station before turning and sprinting the whole way home.

24

A Silent Sacrifice

His heart leapt when he heard a knock at the door. He glanced at himself one more time in the mirror, running his hand through his hair and flashing a smile, searching for confidence in his reflection. Pier Giorgio rolled his eyes at his own insecurities and raced down the stairs. Yet upon opening the door, he was confronted by an unexpected guest.

"Pier Giorgio! You're home!"

He smiled. "Greetings, Signora Converso. And how are you today?"

The elderly woman, hunched so low her eyes were directed toward the floor, hobbled past the doorway and into the Frassati home.

"Oh, Georgie, I'm well, but tired. I seem to always be tired."

"I can sympathize; the race we run is a difficult one, no?" She went on about her aches and pains as Pier Giorgio stole glances out the door and down the street. "And what can I do for you today?"

"I'm so sorry to bother you, but I wanted to come and ask if you would help mend my front door. The lock is broken and I don't feel safe with all these Fascists running about. A lonely woman like me needs to have a door that locks, don't you think?"

"Absolutely," he agreed. "I'm waiting on some guests, but may I run over to your home later today?"

"Oh, of course, Georgie. I knew you would understand. I didn't know who else to ask with Bertone off at holiday."

"And how is he doing?"

She sighed. "Well, I suppose. I wish he'd come to see me more often. I see *you* more than my own son."

"He's a good boy; you did a fine job raising him. Now, I'll see you in a few hours with my tools in hand, and how about I bring you some fresh bread from the market as well?"

"Bless you, Georgie!" she said reaching up to caress his cheek. "Bless you!"

He escorted her down the sidewalk and waved goodbye.

"Who was that?" Luciana asked when he came back inside.

"Signora Converso. She needs help fixing her door."

"Bertone's mother?" He nodded, pulling back the curtain and glancing out the window. "That woman knocks on our door every day. You shouldn't encourage her, Georgie. She will only continue to bother you if you continue to help her."

"She's no bother. Where is mother?"

"Upstairs, getting ready."

"She knows nothing of my feelings for Laura, no?"

"I didn't tell her. Did you?"

"Of course not. I want to gauge her reaction to Laura first; Papa, as well."

The next ten minutes passed in anxious agony. Laura and Christina were late, sending him toward the window on jittery feet every so often. Perhaps they were not coming at all, he thought.

Adelaide came down the stairs a moment later.

"Did I hear someone down here earlier?"

"Georgie's best friend, Signora Converso, came again for a request; this time for him to fix her door."

"That woman is relentless. No shame or pity. You shouldn't keep helping her, Georgie."

"That's what I told him," Luciana confirmed.

Pier Giorgio remained silent.

"Is your father here?" Adelaide asked.

"I believe he's in the study," Luciana answered.

Adelaide moved down the hall and turned into the study. The low drone of their voices, muted by the distance and the walls, came to the Frassati children as they stood in the den. At first the exchange was lifeless and casual, but slowly their voices gained volume, eventually turning into shouts.

Pier Giorgio and Luciana looked to one another with knowing eyes, each feeling the anguish from the growing chasm forging between their parents. The dinner table had become an impending battle each night, but lately their skirmishes had extended to other intervals throughout the day. It was amazing they found so much time to bicker considering how much Alfredo remained at the office. But then, Pier Giorgio thought, perhaps the distance caused the bickering.

Alfredo emerged from the room, throwing his coat over

his shoulders. He walked briskly into the den and toward the front door, oblivious to the presence of his children. Adelaide watched him from the study doorway.

"Papa, you're leaving?" Pier Giorgio asked.

"Yes," he responded without breaking stride.

"But I have invited guests over to have tea. I'd like for you to meet them, and I feel certain they would like very much to meet you. I've told them so much about you."

"I'm sorry, son. I must go."

He left without another word.

Adelaide moved into the kitchen to check on the servants and the state of the tea and breaded cakes they'd serve their guests. Pier Giorgio walked outside and sat on the front stoop of their house. It was early summer and the day was bright and cloudless. But the agreeable weather failed to provide the necessary cheer that might displace the gloom enveloping his heart.

He wanted nothing more than to bring joy and peace to his family, but he seemed to be as helpless in nurturing the harmony of his parents' relationship as he was in controlling the rain clouds. At times, he would spend hours and even days planning a family event, in hopes that the bonding would bring everyone together, only to have his father or mother, or both, cancel.

But what was perhaps most frustrating about his parents' arguments was that their genesis was impossible to trace. No one quite knew, perhaps not even themselves, what they were fighting about. His father's gruffness and driven personality blended with his mother's hypersensitivity and vacillating artistic nature proved to be an ominous concoction that acted like poison to their marriage. Pier Giorgio strived in vain to find the antidote, but there was no certainty one even existed.

"Georgie?"

He looked up. Christina and Laura were standing before him. He jumped to his feet.

"Hello! I'm sorry; I didn't see you walk up."

"Are we that sneaky?" Christina asked Laura.

"We must be."

They both laughed as Pier Giorgio shuffled his feet.

"You both look lovely," he told them, his eyes directed at Laura and her pulled back, dark hair, white sundress, and Miraculous Medal hanging humbly round her neck. The tarnished silver chain and oval-shaped medal belied the glittery jewelry most women in Turin wore. Her well-defined lips curved into a smile, which Pier Giorgio returned.

"Who else is coming?" Christina asked.

"Just the two of you, actually. I invited Mary Amelia, but she was unable to attend."

"So just the women of the Shady Characters were fortunate enough to attend this tea party?" Laura asked. "*Interesting.*"

He blushed but covered nicely. "Yes, so many of my fellow men are chauvinistic, caring little for the delicate feminine flowers of our world, but I strive to care for you women and give you special privileges like my mother's tea."

They giggled.

"I wanted very much to introduce my mother and sister to you ladies today," he went on, "as I tell them so much about our group's adventures into the mountains. I pondered inviting our entire group, but our fellow Shady Characters are not sophisticated enough for afternoon tea. Shall we go inside?"

He ushered them through the door and followed them in. They marveled at the elegance of the Frassati home—its fine, wood-stained floors, pristine furniture, bright chandeliers and exquisite artwork—complimenting Pier Giorgio as they ran their fingers across the mantel, tables, and picture frames with admiration. He thanked them but knew he could take little credit for the nice things within his home.

His mother and Luciana walked confidently into the den.

"Hello," Adelaide said, "you must be Pier Giorgio's friends. How nice of you to visit with us this afternoon."

Pier Giorgio obliged the group with proper introductions, nearly kicking his sister in the shin when she winked at him after meeting Laura. A short tour of the rest of the home ensued, with Adelaide focusing much of the attention on her own artwork scattered about the walls of the house. Laura and Christina followed, voicing their compliments of the various pieces she had painted.

Behind them and alongside his uninterested sister, Pier Giorgio shadowed the three women like a puppy supremely interested in what was happening but powerless to control it. His apprehension reached its peak when they all returned to the den for their tea. The servants had laid out the china cups on top of small plates, circling a silver platter layered with breaded cakes, and were in the process of pouring the tea.

"Where is your father, Georgie?" Laura asked as they all

sat down. "I thought we would be meeting him as well. I'd love to compliment him on his work at *La Stampa*."

"He will not be joining us," Adelaide answered. "Now, Laura, Christina; tell me about yourselves."

Christina hesitated but spoke first, relaying where she had grown up, been educated, and currently lived. She went on pleasantly about her upbringing and interests, but Pier Giorgio heard none of it as he waited for Laura's turn to speak.

"Laura is a student of Mathematics," he suddenly blurted out, cutting Christina off.

Everyone in the room looked to him. Luciana hid her smile behind her cup of tea.

"Let her speak for herself, Georgie," his mother suggested.

Laura nodded and smiled at Pier Giorgio. "Yes, I'm in the process of getting my degree in Mathematics."

"What will you do with that education," Adelaide asked. "As a woman, I mean."

"I wish to be a teacher one day."

"Spend all that time learning just to pass it on?" Adelaide said. "Do you not want to put it to better use?"

"Teaching is a noble profession, Mama," Luciana offered, blowing on her cup of tea.

Adelaide shrugged and said, "And where did you grow up?"

"In Carmagnola, not far from here."

"Is that where your family still lives?"

"No, Signora Frassati, I grew up at an orphanage with my brother."

Adelaide struggled for two long seconds in search of a response.

"Oh, I'm sorry."

"It's alright. I have no bad memories from my childhood. My brother and I enjoyed our time at the orphanage with the other children."

"Where does your brother live now?" Luciana asked.

"With me. We have an apartment near the train station."

The conversation found a lull, at which point Pier Giorgio broke in by telling a story of their latest climb. Adelaide rose and left the room for ten minutes. Luciana entertained the girls while Pier Giorgio went to look for her. He found her in the kitchen staring out the window.

"Mama, are you alright?"

"What?" She turned around. "Oh, yes. What did you say?"

"What are you doing in here? We have guests."

"Yes, I know, but I'm so tired, Georgie."

"Can you just come and visit for a few more minutes?"

They walked back into the den. Pier Giorgio was glad to see Luciana laughing with Laura as they flipped through an old family photo album.

"You were a cute little boy," Laura said.

"And nothing has changed, no?" he said casting a broad smile. He helped his mother to her seat on the couch.

"Humility is the source of your good looks," Luciana offered, "don't ruin it with pride, brother."

"I wouldn't dare it."

The conversation carried on as they flipped through

the album, admiring the passing years of the Frassati family through the black-and-white snapshots. As Laura flipped one of the pages over, she spilled a few drops of tea on a picture of Alfredo and Adelaide taken years ago. Pier Giorgio's mother rose from her spot on the couch and ripped the album away from Laura.

"What have you done?" she asked, wiping the picture with a napkin.

"I'm so sorry!" Laura pleaded. "It was an accident."

"Yes, Mama," Pier Giorgio said walking over to her, "it was an accident."

Adelaide said nothing, looking down into the picture. She and her husband stood on the coast, with the water and a sunset at their backs. Everyone waited for further reaction from her. Finally, she turned and smiled, "It's alright, I know it was an accident. Please excuse me, children, I must go rest. I feel a headache coming on."

She left and walked slowly up the stairs. Luciana said her goodbyes to Laura and Christina and Pier Giorgio walked them out to the street.

"Pier Giorgio, I'm so sorry I spilled tea on that picture."

"Don't worry, Laura, her reaction had more to do with other complicated matters than a little tea spilled on an old picture. I thank you both for coming."

He hugged them and went back inside. Luciana was helping the servants clear away the dishes to the kitchen. Pier Giorgio went upstairs to check on his mother.

"Mama?" he said, gently knocking on her bedroom door.

"Come in."

She lay flat on the bed with a wet cloth over her eyes. He came to her side and sat down on the edge of the bed.

"Can I get you anything, Mama?"

"No, thank you, I just need to rest."

"How did you like my friends?"

"I suppose they were alright, but where do you find these people, Georgie? You come from such privilege, and yet you bring orphans home as your best friends?"

He shrugged. "I meet them from all over."

"We need to find you a good girl from an established family."

"But I enjoy Laura's company."

He realized he hadn't included Christina but didn't care.

"I'm sure you do, but life is too complicated to carry on with orphans and helping poor old ladies fix their doors and staying up half the night saying that rosary of yours. You're almost of age to begin your work at *La Stampa* and you need to take on more responsibility."

Pier Giorgio was at a loss for how to respond. They sat in silence for several minutes, filled only by the chirping of a bird on the windowsill.

"Are you still angry about the picture?" He noticed she still held it in her hand. The tea had stained the top corner of the picture with a circular splotch.

"No, I was never mad about that."

"It was an accident."

"I know. Georgie, listen . . ." she sat up and removed the cloth from her eyes. "You should know that your father has suggested he and I get a separation."

"What?"

"It may be for the best, I don't know, but it's still terribly humiliating. I don't know what to do."

"Mama, you cannot separate."

"That's not for you to say. It is your father's and my decision."

"But . . ."

"I'm just so tired all the time, though," she went on, "it's these headaches, they sap my strength. I told your father I need time to think and rest."

"Does Luciana know?"

"I'll tell her today, after I take my nap. Could you get me a glass of water?" He grabbed the cup on her bedside table and went to the bathroom to fill it up. "Thank you, Georgie. Please shut the door on your way out, and tell Mariscia that I'm sleeping and to not let anyone disturb me."

"Yes, Mama."

He left her room, grabbed his tools, and departed for the other side of town. He stopped to get Signora Converso bread as promised and spent an hour mending the lock on her front door. He hugged her, receiving her warm gratitude with a smile, and walked back home as the evening overtook the day.

Luciana sat on the front stoop of their house staring into nothingness. He knew his mother had delivered her the news.

"I haven't been able to make sense of it either," he said sitting down beside her.

"I suppose it makes perfect sense, if you simply watch them together."

Above them, the stars swept over Turin like glitter as they blinked with brilliance.

"I really liked Laura," Luciana said.

"Good. That means a lot. Thank you."

"What did Mama think of her?"

"I don't think she thought much of her at all."

"You should still tell Laura how you feel. I think she likes you. She watched you all throughout our visit."

"Is that so?"

Luciana nodded.

"That's wonderful to hear, but I cannot pursue anything with Laura right now. My heart aches to say that, but it is the way of things. Mama's health seems to be poor, and with all that is happening between her and Papa, I don't think it wise to add such a burden on her. The drama would be too much. I will have to silence my love for Laura, at least for now. I feel certain Mama would have a heart attack if I told her I wished to court the orphaned girl I brought to tea."

"How could you sacrifice your feelings for Mama's? She would not do the same for you."

Pier Giorgio rose to his feet and gazed up at the stars. "I appreciate you visiting with my friends today, sister. I'm going to bed early tonight; I'm very tired."

He leaned down and kissed the top of her head, walking inside and leaving her alone on the front stoop.

25

Intruders

The chaos and tension inside Pier Giorgio's home mirrored the turmoil in the city streets. Mussolini was within arm's reach of becoming a dictator ruling over all of Italy, sending his secret police into the cities to force his will upon the people. He strove to create a totalitarian state through a series of laws and aggressive enforcement, transforming the country into a one-party political dictatorship. Several murders of key political opponents and even a priest were attributed to Mussolini's thugs, though they denied responsibility.

While Pier Giorgio and several of his friends spoke out about the injustices of Fascism against Holy Mother Church, he was devastated that many other Catholics gave in to "Il Duce," as Mussolini was known by.

The I.P.P. made concessions and compromises in the political landscape, relenting power like a helpless child, and the Catholic paper *Il Momento* lent Mussolini a public endorsement. But perhaps most maddening to Pier Giorgio was the instance when his Catholic Men's Club at the University honored Mussolini by allowing the Fascist flag to be flown in the streets as he and his followers marched

199

through Turin. This act prompted Pier Giorgio's resignation from the Cesare Balbo.

He wrote to the president of the Club:

> I was revolted to hear that this banner, which I have carried so often in religious processions, was displayed by you to pay homage to such a man, a man who has destroyed religious works, has made no attempt to control the Fascists, has allowed ministers of God to be assassinated, has permitted all sorts of other outrages to be committed, and is trying to cover up his misdeeds by replacing the crucifix in the schools. Taking full responsibility on myself, I have removed this banner and I send you herewith my irrevocable resignation. I wish this letter, written in haste, but dictated by the deepest convictions of my soul, to be read at the next meeting.

Pier Giorgio Frassati

The hypocrisy was what angered Pier Giorgio. These groups claimed to be furthering the Church's cause, and yet did not stand up for the decency and righteousness in which they preached.

"These men are like turn signals at railroad tracks," he told his friend Marco. "They do not stand up for themselves, but simply alter their opinion and turn in the direction they're told to. It's a sad day when Catholics cower to evil and treat the teachings of their Church as if they are merely *suggestions*, abandoning them without the slightest sign of a troubled conscious."

Pier Giorgio continued to admire the stance his father took against the Fascists. Together, the two of them did what they could to combat the power of the Black Shirts, though from varying points of view. Pier Giorgio spoke with a passion fueled by his faith as he frequented dozens of religious demonstrations, while Alfredo voiced his concerns from a political stance, writing daily articles in *La Stampa* about the dark road Mussolini was taking their beloved country down. Unfortunately for both of them and their family, the Fascists took notice.

The door bell rang.

"Mariscia," Adelaide called out, "won't you see who that is?"

The Frassati's house servant walked down the hallway, past the dining room where Pier Giorgio and his mother sat eating a late lunch. She cracked the door and with one eye peering outside, noted a well-dressed young man.

He smiled. "Hello, Signora, is Alfredo Frassati in?"

"No, I'm sorry, he's out. May I tell him your name?"

His smile vanished rather sharply. Inexplicably, he turned completely 'round so that his back was to her.

"Signor?" Mariscia questioned. "What may I do for you?"

He nodded and waved to someone on the street, then whipped around and threw his shoulder into the door!

Mariscia's head was thrown back from the blow of the door hitting her face. The man grabbed a truncheon he'd hid beside the door and burst into the house. Mariscia gathered her wits, wiping at the blood dripping from her nose, and screamed for help. He pulled her by her hair out of the foyer and threw her body into the living room wall. A moment later four other men flooded the house, scattering about like roaches to different rooms.

From the dining room, Pier Giorgio heard the commotion. His eyes darted up to meet his mother's. The color in her face drained away.

"Stay here, Mama!"

Pier Giorgio leapt from his chair and turned down the hall. The first intruder had laid his wooden club on the ground and stood by the telephone stationed on the wall just before the staircase. The man reached into his pocket for a pair of scissors and lifted them to the phone's wires to cut them. Pier Giorgio hurled his body down the hallway and speared the man to the ground. Once on top of him, he thrust blow after blow down upon the man.

Adelaide came around the corner of the hallway screaming hysterically.

"Leave him! Pier Giorgio, let him go; we'll run!"

In all corners the sound of destruction tore through the house—a broken vase, a table turned over, a shattered mirror. The other men worried little for their comrade being the recipient of Pier Giorgio's fists as they ripped apart the Frassati home as quickly as they could.

The man below Pier Giorgio finally regained some semblance of control when he thrust his legs into Pier Giorgio's gut. Pier Giorgio fell back to the floor, but immediately reached for the truncheon lying beside him. The intruder's eyes grew wide at the sight of Pier Giorgio waving the club above his head, screaming, "Cowards! Rascals! Where are the rest of you? I'll take you all!"

The first man shuffled and crawled backwards. The rest of them appeared briefly from the other rooms of the house but sprinted for the door when they saw the enraged young man wielding the wooden club in his hand. He took several steps after them but stopped at the sound of his mother's voice.

"Georgie, no! Let them go! They may have a revolver!"

He relented to his mother's wishes and did not chase after them, but chucked the truncheon out the door at the departing intruders.

"Cowards!"

In the distance, halfway down the block, he saw them pile into a black car and speed away.

His focus shifted.

"Where is Mariscia? Did they take her?"

Adelaide shook her head. "Oh, no! No! They couldn't have; we saw them leave."

"Mariscia?" they called out. "Where are you?"

Pier Giorgio heard her grunting from the living room. He sprinted back across the hallway and found her lying on the verge of unconsciousness behind the couch.

"Mother! She's in here! Get me cold rags!"

By now, Italo, the family chauffeur, had heard the uproar and ran up from the cellar. He helped Pier Giorgio lift Mariscia to the couch and there they tended to her wounds as they waited for medical care and the authorities to arrive.

In the coming days, all of Turin read about the invasion of the Frassati home by the Fascists. It was unclear if they had intended only to vandalize the home, or actually cause harm. Alfredo struggled with the fact that he was not there, knowing the men sought him and not his family. Pier Giorgio, though he deflected it, received praise from his father and from other friends and family for his heroism.

"It was merely instincts," he claimed to Luciana who had been off in London at the time. "And even five against one is an easy fight when you are battling against cowardly scoundrels."

Though the entire episode brought a great deal of trauma to his family, Pier Giorgio was thankful for what had happened, at least in one regard. Before retiring to his bedroom for the evening he glanced into his parents' bedroom with the intention of saying goodnight. But upon seeing his father holding his mother as they lay in bed together, his shirt wet with her tears, Pier Giorgio remained silent and watched from the doorway. The serene silence resting within his house brought him a smile. At least on this night, the sound of his parents' arguments would remain foreign to his ears.

26

Goodbyes at the Train Station

Pier Giorgio struggled to assemble himself in the proper attire that would reflect the high society in which the occasion merited. He reached for the set of pearls on his bureau and struggled with stiff fingers to place them inside the button holes of his starched, white shirt.

"Having trouble, Georgie?"

Mariscia stood in the doorway. She walked over and took the pearls from him, setting them inside the holes with ease.

"I don't enjoy the social expectations to wear such clothing. I should give them all to my poor and then I'll have an excuse for not dressing properly."

"And what would the poor need with starched shirts, pearl studs, and dinner jackets?" Mariscia asked as she straightened up his crooked tie and matted down his messy hair.

"A fine point," he admitted, "then we should sell the clothes and give them the money, no?"

"Perhaps after the wedding you can do that, Georgie."

The smile she'd come to expect from him remained hidden. "I know you'll miss her," she added.

"I don't know what I'll do without her around."

"You two have been separated before and been fine. I'm sure this time will be no different."

"She's getting married, Mariscia, and to a man who will take her out of *Italia* and to distant shores. We will be apart now, not for a matter of days, but rather months, only seeing each other on seldom occasions. I have only recently realized what it means to have a sister at home, and what an empty space her leaving creates. Oh, how we take our blessings for granted! Things may never be the same for us. I can hardly bear it."

"You mustn't blame Signor Gawronska for taking her away. His diplomatic duties require that they leave for Holland."

"No, of course not. Jan is a fine man, and Luciana is lucky to have him. I must disguise my sadness and be happy for them today. I only wish they would wed and then he take his leave without her."

She smirked.

"I'm of course kidding, . . . mostly."

"Come, Georgie, it's almost time to leave."

They headed for the door but Pier Giorgio stopped. "I've almost forgotten Luciana's wedding gift." He raced to his closet and retrieved a white box. "Has she left yet?"

"No, I believe she's in her room putting on the final touches."

Pier Giorgio hurried across the hallway and knocked on the door. Behind it he heard his sister and mother arguing about how she should wear her hair. He burst in without invitation.

"You two must stop all this; we know she will be gorgeous no matter her hairstyle."

They ignored him and carried on with the disagreement. He waited patiently before they compromised on something that looked no different than what either of them had suggested in the first place, or so Pier Giorgio thought.

"We leave in five minutes," Adelaide said.

"Your dress is lovely, Mama," he said leaning over to kiss her as she left the room.

"Thank you, Georgie. You too look very fine and handsome. Don't let your sister delay and tinker much longer."

"Yes, Mama."

He turned back to his sister. She stood before him in her wedding gown, glowing beneath the sunlight flooding the window. She cocked her head to the side and shrugged.

"So, how do I look?"

He saw in that moment both the woman she had become, her beauty and elegance, and the innocent child he'd grown up beside throughout the years. He battled his emotions with all his power.

"You have asked me this so many times before, and so many times I've had an answer, but today I cannot find the words to express your beauty."

He walked over and hugged her, clinching his eyes to hold back the tears.

"What's in the box?" she asked when they separated.

"Ah, you've noticed? It's your gift. Do we have time for you to open it?"

"Yes, of course!"

He handed it over and watched as she opened the box and unwrapped the tissue paper, revealing an ivory crucifix.

"Do you like it? I found it in an antique shop."

She hesitated, looking down at the body of Jesus slung upon the cross. "Yes, brother, it's wonderful. How sweet you are."

She hugged him, but he felt reservation in her.

"If you don't like it, I can return it."

"Don't be silly. I'll give it to Mariscia to place with the rest of the gifts. But we must go or Mama will have a heart attack."

The family left for the church and an hour later Archbishop Gamba blessed the union between Luciana Frassati and Jan Gawronska. Pier Giorgio kept a happy façade throughout the entire day, even through the reception dinner as his ears were chewed off by a distant Polish cousin.

To break away from the crowd, he scanned the table where the gifts sat on display. Beneath the white tablecloth, hidden and still wrapped in tissue paper, he found the ivory crucifix he'd given Luciana. He focused on the face of the dying Christ, then glanced back at the table lined with candlesticks, crystal wear, fine china, vases, and silver platters.

"What is that, a crucifix?"

Pier Giorgio turned around. A man swayed back and forth behind him, a wine glass in hand, an inane smile on his face, and food stains crusted to his shirt. "This is a wedding, not a funeral!" He laughed and walked away. Pier Giorgio rewrapped the crucifix and placed it back under the table.

After the reception, the family escorted the couple to the train station where they would depart for their honeymoon. Luciana hugged both her parents before facing Pier Giorgio.

"It'll not be long before I see you again," she said. He nodded and wiped at his eyes but remained silent. "Georgie, you're never at a loss for words. Say something to me before I climb aboard this train."

Still, Pier Giorgio faltered for words. Luciana noticed his hands were trembling. She turned to her husband.

"Jan, why don't you go ahead? I'll come find you."

She nodded toward her parents. They understood and kissed her one last time before walking away. Only brother and sister remained. Pier Giorgio finally surrendered to his emotions and threw his arms around her. He sobbed onto her shoulder; Luciana's eyes too ran wet with tears.

"Georgie, why have you done this to me? I cannot cry like this on my wedding day."

"I'm sorry," he bellowed, still buried in her coat. "But I don't know if I can be alone with the two of them. Their bickering drains all that's in me. They jump for each other's throats but it's me who feels like I'm suffocating."

"They've been better lately. It will be okay."

"I've prayed that they will love each other once again, but I've begun to fear my prayers fall upon the deaf ears. How dare I doubt our Lord, but I cannot help but think this way after seeing them deteriorate for so many years."

"It's not your fault, Georgie. You cannot control their love or behavior toward one another. Continue with your prayers, which I know make you so happy; that's all you can do."

"You see," he said, finally backing away, "what beautiful advice. What will come of me without you, my best friend, by my side?"

She laughed through her tears. "You will never have a shortage of friends. This much, I know."

"But it's only you who understands, Luciana. Only you."

She pulled him to her again but found no further words of comfort to offer. He finally composed himself and backed away, wiping at his eyes and nose.

"I am terribly sorry. This display I've put on was not fair to you, not today on this your most special day. Please accept my apologies."

"Oh, hush. You and I are beyond such formal apologies. You know I'll visit often, don't you?"

"Yes, you must. And write every day."

"Every day?"

"Yes, promise, at least for the first month."

"Okay, sweet Georgie, you sentimental fool. I will write you each day for the next month. I promise."

He kissed her on the cheek. "Go now, sister. I love you."

"And you."

She turned and walked away, waving one last time before disappearing onto the train. As she fell from sight Pier Giorgio began to cry again, wishing the two of them could return to the sequoia tree they once climbed in their Pollone garden.

27

The Banishment of Gloom

On a spring day in 1925 Pier Giorgio awoke with the intention of spending the day studying for one of his final exams. The long road of his education at the Polytechnic, delayed several times by his time in Germany and other commitments he'd made to so many organizations, was finally nearing an end. The winding caverns of his journey through the world of his mining classes were giving way to the light of completion. Soon, he would obtain his degree and journey into the *actual* hollows beneath the mountains, making a dream once foreign to him a concrete reality.

But as he found his way into the kitchen to grab a quick bite of breakfast, he saw a note waiting on him:

> Georgie, come see me at the office.
>
> Papa

Though stressed by his impending exam, he got dressed and walked outside. He paused to greet the police officers who had held rotating shifts outside their home since the Fascists attacked. Pier Giorgio gave them some bread and paused to speak with them awhile, then took the train over to the office of *La Stampa* to see his father, bringing along his books so he could journey to the library afterwards. He was greeted as usual by smiles and hugs as he strolled through the building toward his father's office. Some of these people had watched him grow up and looked at him and his sister as the honorary children of *La Stampa*.

On the top floor in the corner office, he poked his head past the door. His father was not in. Pier Giorgio walked next door to the office of his father's right-hand man, Signor Cassone.

"Pier Giorgio!" He rose and greeted him in the doorway. "How wonderful it is to see you. Have you been well?"

"Yes, it's fine to see you, too. How is your family?"

"Crazy as ever, but all in good spirits."

"Wonderful. Is my father in? He left a note to come see him."

"He's left town for the day—a big meeting."

"Oh, alright."

"But he told me you'd be by. Won't you come with me?" He put his arm around Pier Giorgio and escorted him down the hall. "Did you walk over or catch the train?"

"I rode the train. I must move quickly today so I can prepare for my exams."

"Your father tells me you always ride third-class. It baffles him, me as well."

"I ride third because there's no fourth."

"I'm not sure that's an answer."

Pier Giorgio shrugged. "I feel more comfortable there."

Signor Cassone smiled. They turned a corner and stopped before an unoccupied office. An oak desk rested before a window—a lamp, typewriter, pens and accounting books sitting atop it and a wooden chair placed under it. A file cabinet stood in one corner and a coat and hat rack in the other. Three walls were bare, while the last held a painting of a mountain range. Signor Cassone held out his hand.

"Go ahead," he said.

"I'm sorry, I don't understand."

"It's yours." He took off Pier Giorgio's hat and hung it on the rack. "Have a seat."

Pier Giorgio slowly walked through the doorway behind him. Signor Cassone pulled out the chair for him. He sat down.

"What do you think, Georgie?"

"I'm afraid I am still confused."

"This is going to be your office. You'll start work here next month."

"What? But . . ."

"What's the problem?"

"I had no idea."

"No?"

Pier Giorgio shook his head. "I'll complete my mining engineering degree in just a few short weeks. I plan to start a career in this field."

"Is this something you've discussed with your father?"

"Yes, he knows about the pursuit of my degree. I thought perhaps I would volunteer here a few days a month, but never did I intend to come full-time to *La Stampa*."

Signor Cassone sighed, walking slowly across the room and running his hand through his black hair. He leaned against the windowsill and peered over to Pier Giorgio.

The young man's eyes bore the innocent confusion of a child.

"I didn't want to tell you all this today. Your father left abruptly and told me to 'handle it.' I wonder if he even had a meeting, or if he just wanted to avoid this conversation."

"I'm sorry?"

"Georgie, this desk has been picked out for you since your birth. I know you were studying for a different career, but your father has always known this awaited you."

"But I've spent so much time studying and working toward my degree."

Signor Cassone pursed his lips and shrugged. "I'm not sure that makes much of a difference to him. He wants so badly for you to take over his duties here. He wants a Frassati to always run *La Stampa*. You're his son, Georgie, his namesake."

A long pause ensued. Pier Giorgio's head hung toward the ground before turning to gaze at the painting of the mountains. Signor Cassone felt the pangs of guilt when he saw a slow tear creep down Pier Giorgio's cheek.

"So it will please Papa if I come to work here?"

". . . I'm sure it will, Georgie."

He nodded. "Then I accept." Pier Giorgio rose and extended his hand. "It will be an honor to work alongside you, Signor Cassone."

"Yes, and you. But I'm sorry; I know this is not what you want."

Pier Giorgio smiled. "What the Lord wants is all that's important."

He left the office and returned home, forgoing his

studies. An hour later he was on his way to a nearby park to meet his friend, Isidoro. Pier Giorgio had called his dear friend, begging for companionship, and Isidoro had heard the desperation in his voice. Isidoro phoned in sick to his job and met Pier Giorgio at a bench in the park where they sat eating a picnic lunch.

After minutes in casual conversation, Isidoro said, "Georgie, you seem down. What's bothering you?"

Pier Giorgio told him what had happened.

"My, this is most troubling to hear. Does your father not understand all the work you've put in to get your engineering degree?"

"A part of him may understand, but only subconsciously. I have begun to realize he tolerated my other career aspirations but never took them seriously. It seems he always knew I would join him at the paper full-time."

"Is there a part of you that regrets all the work you've done? Do you wish you'd gone to work there years ago?"

"No," he answered without hesitation. "I've learned many interesting things in my studies, and met special people. I could never regret my path, nor predict where it will take me next. Perhaps everything I learned will be put to use later."

"I always wondered why you chose such a field—mining engineering."

"It can be interesting work, but mostly I wanted to assist these workers in their daily struggle. They have a difficult calling in the mines, and to make matters worse, they've been exploited for years. I thought if I was able to obtain a managerial position I could make a difference."

"I know all that, Georgie. But with how passionate you are with your faith, I always figured you would become a missionary."

"At one point I thought this as well. My heart certainly finds joy in missionary work. But the pursuit of my degree is linked to my mission work; it always has been. I find the discipline I learn from my studies helps in the formation of my mission life. And anyway, my parents would never allow me to be a full-time missionary. Any schooling I did, even though it was not leading me toward *La Stampa*, kept them happy, allowing me to visit and help whomever I could without the gaze of their watchful eye. My studies have always served such purposes for me. I'm sad it appears I will not be able to put all this knowledge to use, but am thankful for these last few years nonetheless."

They ate their sandwiches in silence for several minutes. A mother walked by with a crying baby in a stroller. All they could see were the infant's feet poking up into the air.

"You have had a tough go of it lately, Georgie. As your friend, this makes me sad."

"What do you mean?"

"Your parents' difficulties, your love for Laura that tears you apart, and now this."

Not many people were privy to the personal matters of Pier Giorgio's life, but Isidoro was.

Pier Giorgio nodded and smiled. "I thank you for your kind words, but perhaps I've been whining too much to you about these things. The fact that you're such a good friend apparently serves as a temptation for me to bemoan my misfortunes. But today, in the struggle, I can only thank God, who in his infinite mercy desires to give me all this heartache, so that through these difficulties I might return to a more spiritual interior life. Besides, I'm not truly sad, at least not on the grand scale. On the grand scale, I am filled with bliss."

"The grand scale?"

"Yes, a Christian can never *truly* be sad, Isidoro. How is this possible, when the end that awaits us overpowers all the sadness in the world like a tidal wave coming ashore? As long as faith gives me strength I will always be joyful, and every one of us should feel this way. Sadness and gloom ought to be banished from Catholic souls. One can certainly be hurt at times; we all have been. But we cannot allow a perpetual depression to plague us, for the gloom of depression should not be able to find our soul. My life is monotonous and difficult, but each day I understand a little better the incomparable grace of being a Catholic—days like this prove this more than others. Of course I'm upset about the future my father has planned for me, but down with my melancholy. What, in the grand scheme of life, does this melancholy mean in comparison to the eternity of bliss that awaits me if I maintain the faith Christ asks of us? Gloom should never take root except in the heart which has lost the Faith."

"I admire your attitude," Isidoro replied. "I don't always have such an outlook when troubled times come to me."

"That is part of the struggle, to fight against our natural tendency toward unhappiness. It is within us because we are fallen. But our life, in order to be Christian, has to be a continual renunciation, a continual sacrifice. However, this is not difficult if one thinks, what are these few years passed in suffering compared with eternal happiness, where joy will have no measure nor end, and we shall have unimaginable peace. We should grasp faith strongly. Without it, what would our whole life be? Nothing. It would have been spent in vain. The faith given to me in baptism suggests one thing of which I have no doubt: of yourself you will do nothing, but if you have God as the center of all your action, then you will reach the goal."

"And what is the goal?"

"Happiness, of course, and peace and joy. We must strive for a quiet spirit that yearns for nothing more than to be with God." Pier Giorgio paused. "And there is perhaps one more goal we should have?"

Isidoro turned to him.

"To have some of your mother's world-famous sausage for dinner tonight? I think this is the best way for me to obtain inner peace and joy. What do you say to that?"

They laughed, rose, and departed from the park bench, smiling beneath the sun.

28

To the Heights

The month of June, 1925 brought forth temperate weather that met agreeably with those who wished to climb to the heights. On this, the 7th of the month and the first Sunday, Pier Giorgio set out with his friend Guido Unterrichter to the peaks of La Lunelle. He attended a Mass which ran long, delaying his arrival to the train station.

They rode northwest to Pessinetto Station and exited the train, leaving for higher stratospheres with a brisk walk. Their hike stretched pleasantly before them at first, gradual inclines met easily with plain steps. Mountain cottages where climbers could stay were stationed sporadically on the banks, but the two young men passed them by with the intention of reaching summits where mankind became alien.

The time was perfect for the blooming of life on the mountainside. Patches of rhododendrons perfumed their path on either side and they made plans to gather what they could on their descent. Upon reaching the crest of a hill, they had hoped to make out the peak of Lunelle, but a slow-roaming storm cloud shrouded their view as it overtook the mountain. It began to rain and so they unpacked their water gear and moved onward.

In time, they approached the steep cliffs and gorges for which the challenge was taken. Pier Giorgio led, a rope harnessed between them. They navigated through a narrow pass they anticipated would take them toward the peak, but their way was confused by the cloudy weather and questionable suggestions earlier from a guide on the ground. Despite the uncertainty, they kept pace in good spirits, admiring the rolling terrain below and the fellowship of each other's good-natured company.

They paused for a break to eat and regain their strength, at which point Pier Giorgio brought to mind a fellow student at the Polytechnic, Cesarino Rovere, who had died on this slope in 1921. He suggested they recite a *De Profundis* for the eternal peace of his soul and so they did:

"Out of the depths have I cried to thee, O Lord. Let your ears be attentive to my voice in supplication. If you, O Lord, mark iniquities, Lord, who can stand? But with you is forgiveness, that you may be revered. I trust in the Lord; my soul trusts in His word. My soul waits for the Lord more than sentinels wait for the dawn. More than sentinels wait for the dawn, let Israel wait for the Lord, for with the Lord is kindness and with Him is plenteous redemption; And he will redeem Israel from all their iniquities."

At rising once more, the storm which had brought rain off and on for the last two hours was swept away by the northern winds. Their view beneath them cleared and brought forth the sight of red and purple flowers contrasting the green hills, mixing like paint on an artist's palette. But upward their heads turned to complete their desired goal.

The greatest obstacle met them in the form of a steep cliff rising at a 90-degree angle and stretching over 100 kilometers, dissolving the good humor that had hitherto accompanied their journey. They scaled it at great peril, doubling their ropes and harnesses. Doubt crept into their spirits, though they did not speak of this for fear of thieving each other's confidence.

However, once past the spurs of the crest they embraced in common joy of their accomplishment. A spring within their souls flowed steadily with the waters of peace that all mountain climbers felt upon reaching the summit. Together they rested in silence before the panorama, afflicted with the blessing of amnesia as the stresses of the world below departed from their memory as simply as a breeze flowing through an open window.

Their descent began with a sense of both relief and melancholy at the journey that had come to pass. Pier Giorgio knew each climb could not last forever, though he wanted it so, and yet still he looked forward to returning home. This paradox befuddled him.

"All I seem to think of while home amidst the slowness of daily life is the next chance I'll have to journey into these mountains," he said to Guido, "and yet, once here, I look with favor upon my return. How fickle our desires are; will we never be happy in this life? I think not. But coming up here I realize the importance of our daily lives at home, despite how tedious they might be. It's that comforting uniformity and normality that paves the way for my appreciation of not just these mountain adventures, but also the wonder of God, for it's this contrast which allows for the admiration of the divine. And so let us return to our families, Guido, but let us not return empty-handed; I must bring back some of these flowers for Mama!"

At plucking a few rhododendrons, Pier Giorgio came to realize that just a few wouldn't do. He dug up an entire bush, roots intact, and stuffed it carefully down into his rucksack. They hurried on their way as the coming of night pursued them, arriving at the cottages just as darkness cloaked their eyes. They ate a meal, reminiscing on their climb, and enjoyed a box of spiced cookies Pier Giorgio had brought with him. Before retiring for the night, Pier Giorgio led them in saying the Rosary. The slumber that ensued was as deep as the ocean, filled by the currents of vivid dreams that flow through the mind when exhaustion sets in.

When the sun returned, they rose and gathered their things, journeying to the train station and reaching it by lunchtime. On the ride back to Turin they enjoyed a bottle of red wine, emptying it by the time they arrived. The flow of wine and good spirits sprung them into song as they walked back through the streets of Turin. Pier Giorgio, as usual, cared little for the deficiencies of his tones and sang louder than Guido, drowning out the pleasant voice of his companion. A group of children stopped them and asked if they could have some of the flowers they'd brought back from Lunelle. Pier Giorgio and Guido obliged and commanded that they take them straight home to their mothers.

At their departure, they embraced and promised to repeat their adventure in the coming weeks. Pier Giorgio

went on his way, turning for home to plant the rhododen-
dron bush in the garden for his mother. Once through
the door, though, an overwhelming feeling of fatigue consumed him. It was beyond the normal exhaustion following his climbs, and by nightfall the weariness turned to
pain, clinging to his muscles as the night came and went.

29

Flowers by the River

Pier Giorgio waved to the smiling faces glued to the window of the Provincial Institute for Children. Small circles of fog clouded the window where their breath met the glass. Pier Giorgio zeroed in on two of his favorite orphans standing before the other children, best friends named Antonio and Paolo. He winked at them and smiled; they giggled and winked back.

On his way home near the center of Turin he passed Father Righini, a priest and friend from a nearby parish. They spoke amicably, until in a single moment Pier Giorgio's expression turned cold and hollow.

"What is it, Georgie?"

"Father, I must make my confession."

"Now?"

"Yes, please."

"But Holy Martyrs is just down the road. Surely someone can hear your confession there? Or I could take you there and hear it if you wish?"

"No, it must be here, and now."

Father Righini nodded and together they walked to a nearby bench.

"In the name of the Father, the Son, and the Holy Spirit," they said together.

"Forgive me Father for I have sinned, it has been nearly two weeks since my last confession . . ."

Pier Giorgio made his confession and listened intently to his penance. When they rose from the bench, Father Righini said, "That is the first confession I've heard on the busy city streets. What was the meaning of this urgency?"

"Something came over me. I knew it had to be done now."

The priest noted the fatigue draining Pier Giorgio's normal vitality, and the paleness of his complexion.

"Are you alright, Georgie? You do not look well."

"Yes, I'm fine. I'm just saddened about the state of my beloved grandmother's health. She's fading with each day."

"I'm sorry to hear that. I will keep her in my prayers."

"Yes, thank you."

"Speaking of prayers, mine and yours may have been answered. A possible donor has come forward and may give us a large sum to complete the building of our new rectory. Isn't that wonderful?"

"Indeed, it is. Perhaps the only thing better would be if *many* contributed rather than one."

"What's the difference if the rectory is completed?"

"It's always better when many partake in the giving process. I used to say I would rather collect one lira a hundred times than a hundred lire at once, because in this way the acts of charity are multiplied, and so are acts of humility."

"Ah, well said. I should get you to write my next sermon," he quipped.

Pier Giorgio smiled but was drained by the small-talk. "No, you're a fine priest with superb sermons. But I must return home to check on my grandmother. Goodbye then, Father."

He moved across town but had to stop twice to sit down. The muscles in his legs ached; they felt as if someone were twisting and clinching them, as if they were a wet towel and someone was trying to ring out the water. He massaged them but that brought little relief.

As he entered through the door of his home, he felt the stale presence of human sickness. Grandmother Ametis had taken a turn for the worse in the last nights, surrendering to the passing of her many years. The entire home rested in silence, clutched by the agonizing inevitability of her death—the servants rarely spoke, his mother's face remained red from perpetual tears, smiles were seldom seen, and few found sleep as they all waited. The only joy brought forth from these somber moments was that Luciana would arrive later in the day from Holland to say her goodbyes to Grandmother Ametis. It would mark the first time Pier Giorgio had seen his sister since her wedding day.

He tried to eat lunch but felt queasy. Minutes later he was vomiting up what little food he had in his stomach. It was the third time he had vomited in the last week. Plagued by fatigue, he climbed into bed and fell asleep reading a book on the life of St. Catherine of Siena.

Hours later, he awoke, feeling slightly better. He moved down the hall and poked his head into the guest room they were using to care for his grandmother. The lights were off but glimmers of sunlight filtered through the crack in the closed curtains. Adelaide sat in a chair by the bed, fast asleep beside her mother. Pier Giorgio woke her.

"Mama," he whispered. "Go down and get some dinner. I'll sit with her."

She smiled and left the room. He sat holding his grandmother's hand amidst the dimness, speaking though she couldn't hear.

"Please don't leave me," he whispered. "You're the only one who shines with the Faith. What will come of me and this family without you here?"

He cried quietly into the pillow, but a rush of sickness came over him. He sprinted to the nearby bathroom and barely made it in time. Afterwards he returned to his grandmother's bedside and cried even harder.

"I don't know what's wrong with me. I'm terrified, Grandmother. What has taken over my body?"

With his head buried in the pillow beside her, she lifted her hand and caressed his head. He shot up, meeting her eyes in the darkness.

"Grandmother Ametis, you're awake."

She spoke not, but nodded. Her hand, trembling, rose to her lips. With her fingers she transferred a kiss to his forehead and smiled, then closed her eyes once more.

"Yes," he said through his tears, ". . . oh, sweet lady, return to your dreams. I'll be asleep soon as well and we will meet on the banks of the river and pick flowers. Meet me there. Do you hear me, Grandmother? Meet me by the riverbank in your dreams."

Downstairs, he heard voices of greeting. He recognized

the feel of his sister's presence in the home. He kissed Grandmother Ametis on the cheek and went to see Luciana, wiping at his eyes as he descended the steps.

When he saw his sister, they exchanged a knowing smile, both missing one another but mindful of the somber reasons she had returned home.

"How is she?" Luciana asked.

"She's peaceful," he answered, walking across the room to her. "It's good to see you, sister."

When he entered the light of the den, Luciana said, "Georgie, you do not look well." She hugged him and felt the fatigue in his clutch.

"Just a little cold," came his reply. "I'm fine."

"Does a cold cause you to lose weight? You look spindly."

"I *have* lost my appetite, but come, let me take you to her."

He ushered her up the stairs but gave her time alone with Grandmother Ametis. Pier Giorgio wanted to stay awake and visit with Luciana after her long trip home, but not an hour later he climbed into bed and fell asleep, searching for a river that could flow across dreams.

30

Three Falls

In the morning, Mariscia came into Pier Giorgio's room to retrieve the laundry, never thinking to knock on the door. She jumped when movement came from underneath the covers.

"Oh, Georgie, I'm sorry! I assumed you were up and at Mass."

He glanced at the clock on his bedside. "Normally, you'd be right," he agreed. "Laziness is the biggest fault of young men, isn't it? I'm sorry to have startled you. But I must hurry to make the later Mass; today is the feast of Sts. Peter and Paul. I cannot miss such a special day."

She left him so he could wash and change. After Mass, he and Luciana left to visit a cousin who was on the verge of entering a convent. It was good to relieve themselves of the sorrow and grief consuming the house and enjoy the summer sun.

"Nice of you to wait up and visit with me last night," Luciana said mockingly as they entered the train station. They had planned to walk but Pier Giorgio requested that they take the train due to his poor health.

"I'm sorry, but I told you I do not feel well. I thought

if I went to bed early that would help."

"Did it?"

"Yes, thank you, I'm feeling much better."

"You don't look better. Are you sure you shouldn't go see a doctor?"

"No, Mama already has enough worry with grandma."

After visiting their cousin, they returned home. In the kitchen, Esher, their cook, commented too on the paleness of his color.

"No, I'm fine, but I'll take some aspirin for this headache."

He left the house to avoid anyone else commenting on his declining appearance, saying the Rosary on his way to meet a friend. He went out on a boat on the Po River with Ernesto Atzori, attempting to free his mind from the stresses back home. As they drifted with the current, Pier Giorgio turned to his friend and asked how he looked.

"Not well, actually. Pale and thin."

"Oh, well, I feel fine."

He had hoped Ernesto would give a different answer to assuage the worry concerning his health. Back home, he ate dinner with his father, who was the first person to not comment on Pier Giorgio's appearance in the last day or so. Retiring to his room, he attempted to study for the last two of his exams at the Polytechnic, but was too drained from the activity of the day. He surrendered once again to the fatigue and climbed into bed.

In the depths of the night, he awoke with a fear that his grandmother had passed. He rose in his pajamas and threw a blanket over his shoulders, combating a shiver that ran across his body despite the warmth of the summer night. In the hallway, he stumbled beneath the weight of his own body, but rose and carried onward as quietly as he could. Twice more he fell, three times in all, before reaching his grandmother's side. He grabbed her wrist to feel for her pulse. It was there. In the darkness he prayed for the journey that awaited her.

He slept in again until hearing voices down the hall. His father was confronting his mother with the truth— Grandmother Ametis would not make it through another night.

"I'll fetch a priest," Pier Giorgio offered.

He changed as quickly as he could, though his aching body slowed him. Down the street he moved to the nearby church. No priests were present and so he left an urgent message with a nun praying in the back pew. After returning home, he tried to eat but couldn't stomach anything. He returned to bed for a nap.

When he awoke, he returned to the guest room where his family sat around the bed.

"Have we heard from any of the priests?"

"One was just here," Luciana answered. "Grandmother has received Extreme Unction."

"What?" he asked. "Why didn't you wake me?"

"You still seem ill," Luciana said defensively. "We wanted to let you rest."

"No!" Pier Giorgio broke down on the ground, pounding the floor with his fists. He sobbed so loudly the servants came up the stairs to see about the commotion. "How could you exclude me from such a moment? I should've been there!"

"Calm down, Georgie!" his father commanded. "Get yourself together, she has not died yet. Don't make this worse for your mother. Luciana, get him out of here."

His sister helped him rise from the ground, tears welling in her own eyes at the sight of her ever-joyful brother so distraught. She helped him back into bed, but before she could leave the room he leapt into the bathroom to vomit. She took a step toward him, but hesitated.

"Georgie, I'll get Mariscia to come check on you."

"No," he said through the door. "I'm fine."

She left the room to the sound of his whimpers echoing against the bathroom walls. Before the clock struck midnight, Grandmother Ametis had taken her last breath.

31

Staying Behind

"Mama," Luciana pleaded, "he is too ill. He cannot come to the burial. And you are exhausted from so many nights at the bedside of Grandmother. The two of you should stay here."

The family sat around the den planning the next twenty-four hours. Adelaide sighed.

"So Georgie, again you find a way to bring me stress. Why does it seem impossible that you cannot be there for us when you're needed?"

"Mama," Luciana broke in, "don't say such a thing. He cannot help how sick he is."

"I'm sorry, Mama," Pier Giorgio said from the couch where he lay. Sweat dripped down his forehead but he shivered beneath a sea of blankets. "You can leave me and go, I'll be alright."

"No," Luciana said from across the room. "You seem to be getting worse, not better. Someone must stay here with you. We should phone for Dr. Alvazzi."

"That man has been here long enough in the last days because of Grandmother Ametis," Alfredo said sipping on his brandy. "Give him a rest. If Georgie is not better by next week he can come back. Take another aspirin, son."

"You're giving in," Adelaide said to Pier Giorgio. "You're incapable of making an effort on your own. If you want to get better, you must make the effort."

"Yes, Mama."

Italo, the family driver, did call for a doctor later in the day. Pier Giorgio confessed that his body hurt so much it was difficult for him to sleep. Dr. Alvazzi gave him several sleeping pills that would help him rest through the night and promised to check back in on him the next day. He had not seen a fever quite like this and was worried for the boy. He asked that someone in the family check on him throughout the night.

Alfredo and Adelaide remained silent.

"I had a difficult trip getting here," Luciana confessed. "I'd like to get some sleep before the long day tomorrow."

Just then, Mario Gambetta, a cousin staying in the house from out of town, entered the room. "I'll check in on Pier Giorgio. It's no bother."

Throughout the night, Mario walked down the hall to check on his cousin. Only once was he awake, staring at the ceiling. "Are you okay, Georgie?"

No reply came.

"Georgie, can I get you something?"

His head lifted in the moonlight cascading through the window. "Ah, dear cousin, how sweet you are to check on me. If you could just hand me my rosary, I'd be very grateful."

Mario searched the desk across the room for the Rosary.

"No, it's here, on the bedside."

He walked across the room and grabbed the black beads not a foot from Pier Giorgio. As he handed them over, he noted the odd movements of Pier Giorgio's arm and hand as he went to accept the Rosary. His moves were stilted, as if he were a wooden doll.

"Thank you, Mario. You're too kind. Now return to your rest. You're on holiday right now and should be sleeping. I'll be fine. Don't bother checking on me again."

In the morning, the cortege of cars arrived to take Grandmother Ametis to Pollone. The house hummed with activity as the family and servants prepared themselves for the day ahead. Adelaide went into Pier Giorgio's room, finding him still in bed despite the late hour. His appearance startled her—skin stretched tightly across his bones and as white as the sheets, eyes sunken within his skull, strands of hair fallen onto his pillow, and a foul smell hanging in the room.

"My dear child, do not be so ill. I'm afraid."

"I'm alright, Mama. But I believe Luciana is right; I'm too weak to go today. Oh, please will you and Grandmother forgive me. I have never felt such guilt in my life."

Adelaide looked him over, stricken with worry. She opened her mouth to speak, but was interrupted by a voice from the hallway. One of the servants needed a question answered about the food for the wake.

"I'll be right there," she hollered. Turning back to Pier Giorgio, she said, "I'll stay here with you. Someone must stay here with you."

"No, Mama, you must go. Mariscia is not attending the funeral; she'll stay here with me."

"I'll hear nothing of it. I'm staying with my son."

After she left, Luciana poked her head through the door.

"We're leaving for the funeral. I'll see you when we return, alright?"

"Please double your prayers on account of my absence."

Everything within Pier Giorgio wanted to hug her, but he withheld from requesting that she walk across the room to see him. Instead, he remained silent. She left from her perch in the doorway and fell from sight.

Pier Giorgio dove into a sea of dreams, awaking for several minutes at a time but struggling to grasp consciousness between his moments of slumber. His mind's grip on reality began to loosen, letting go of simple matters—where he was, what his name was, why he was lying in bed—then, as if a switch was flipped, it would all return to him.

Mariscia came in an hour later to check on him, taking his temperature and dabbing his head with a damp cloth.

"When was the last time you ate?"

Pier Giorgio coughed.

"Not long ago, perhaps late last night."

"Don't lie to me."

"I wouldn't dare it," he said with a smile. "Where is Mama?"

"She is in your grandmother's room."

"No, you must get her out of there. Her sadness will overwhelm her. Tell her to come see me; perhaps I can cheer her up. This must be the reason the Lord kept us both from the funeral, so I can keep her mind occupied and cheerful."

Mariscia fetched her.

"Poor Mama," Pier Giorgio said as she entered the room. "Such a difficult time you've had, and here I am bringing you more worry. What a horrible son you have, dear Mama."

"I'm fine; just a little rest is all I need."

She sat at the chair before the desk.

"Mama, have you painted much lately?"

"No, very little, even before Grandmother Ametis fell ill."

"Why?"

"I've not felt the spring of inspiration, I suppose."

"Mama, you must start to paint again. I can see this is when you are at your happiest. What can I do to give you inspiration? Can I tell you that I love you and you're the best mother in the world?"

She smiled. "Yes, Georgie, I am filled with inspiration now."

And so they sat together, mother and son, speaking of everyday matters for over an hour. It was the longest the two of them had spoken in years. Pier Giorgio told her all about his most recent trips into the mountains, and bemoaned his struggles with the studying he still had left, hoping that he could get an extension from his teachers on account of his poor health. She reminisced on memories of her late mother, touching on parts of her childhood that Pier Giorgio had never been privy to, and mused about the future and what awaited her and Alfredo.

"I must lie down," she finally said when their conversation found a pause.

She moved toward the bed and sat on the edge, leaning her head down toward the pillow.

"No!"

She shot back up, alarmed at the volume and energy in his voice which had been absent in the last days.

"You mustn't get so close to me. You might catch this horrible fever."

"Mothers do not catch sicknesses from their children; they are immune."

"Even still, Mama."

She stood back up. "I'm phoning Dr. Alvazzi again."

An hour later, the doctor joined them in the room. He talked to Pier Giorgio about the latest climb into the mountains he'd taken with his son. Pier Giorgio listened with a smile, offering to take them up even further into the clouds as soon as he had recovered.

"If you climb with me, you will look down upon heaven," he claimed.

The doctor laughed. "That may be. Now, let's examine you to see if we can get you well."

Dr. Alvazzi asked him a series of short questions, noting the answers on a notepad. Adelaide listened intently from the other side of the bed. She asked, "What does that mean?" with each answer Pier Giorgio gave, but Dr. Alvazzi fiddled with his mustache and ignored her.

He stopped with his questions and examined Pier Giorgio, peering into his ears, eyes, and mouth. He then pulled the sheet down and began to squeeze his legs. Pier Giorgio winced and Dr. Alvazzi noticed his pain.

"Get up," he commanded of the young boy. Pier

Giorgio remained still. His eyes began to water. "Get up, son."

"Georgie," his mother said, baffled by her son's resistance to such a simple command, "stand up."

"I can't, Mama. I'm sorry, I cannot move."

And he cried.

32

Waiting out the Storm

Luciana sat beside her father at the Pollone cemetery, listening to the priest bless the body of her grandmother. She felt guilty as her mind wandered back to trivial matters and tried to refocus on the ceremony. She thought of the request of her brother to pray twice as much on account of his absence, but soon her mind floated away again, lost in the haze of the Latin prayers flowing from the priest's mouth.

She peered about the cemetery at the tombstones dotting the land and the forest surrounding the grounds like a shell of foliage. Other than the priest, all she could hear was the chirping of birds across the way.

But the sight of a man in a dark suit walking briskly from the parking lot caught her attention. He walked without hesitation past the mourners toward her father.

"Probably an important political matter my father must know about," Luciana thought to herself. She watched as the man pulled Alfredo aside, taking note of his shaken expression. Alfredo remained on the outskirts of the gathering until the ceremony ended.

Luciana walked to him at once.

"Papa, what is it? What's happened?"

Dazed, he stared toward the ground.

"Papa?"

He snapped to attention.

"Luciana, we must return to Turin at once. It's Pier Giorgio."

Next, her father's voice slowed and landed like a bomb when he uttered the word "poliomyelitis." The world fell silent, only filled by the slight ringing in her ears caused by the shock of what she had heard.

As the world returned, she screamed in horror and nearly fell to the ground, caught only by the arms of her father. Others passed by unfazed, thinking her sorrow stemmed from the death of her grandmother.

They walked to the car and drove straight back to Turin. Specialists and nurses had descended upon the house, blitzing it with their knowledge, medicine, and opinions. Alfredo had made several urgent calls around the country asking what could be done, demanding that his son be given everything necessary for his recovery.

Luciana ran upstairs and entered Pier Giorgio's room just as several doctors were leaving to deliver Alfredo their report.

"Georgie, this can't be so!"

She fell to the ground, kneeling by his bedside. He turned his head, slowly, toward her and smiled. He attempted to speak but faltered.

"Don't, save your strength."

Luciana rubbed his hair, brushing it back from his eyes.

"No," Pier Giorgio managed to say, his voice scratchy

and barely intelligible. "Don't touch me."

"Stop it. Stop, let me help you."

She ran to the bathroom to rewet the cloth, dabbing it on his forehead. He shook his head and pointed toward the desk.

"What? What is it, Georgie?"

"My coat pocket . . . please . . ."

She grabbed the coat, checking in the pocket and finding a receipt from a pawn shop and several medical injections.

"What is this?"

"A dear friend of mine, Signora Costa, she . . ." he stopped to cough. "She sold her wedding ring to obtain money to feed her children. I was angered she did not come to me for this, but to fix things I went to the pawn shop to repurchase it. If she takes this receipt there, they will return it to her. Will you take it to the St. Vincent de Paul Center? They'll get it to her, . . . and these injections, they are for a sick man I know, Converso, take them as well to the center. With your help, I'll write a note explaining all this."

Luciana, overcome further in her grief from such a routine yet profound request, began to sob even more as she walked to the desk to retrieve a pen and paper. She placed it in his hands and watched him struggle to find the strength to write just a few simple words. In the end, she helped him sign his name.

"So you will deliver this?" he asked.

"Yes . . . alright, I'll do it, Georgie."

She left to find her parents and discover what would

come of her brother. They sat in the den with Mariscia and several doctors.

"Mama, Papa, what will happen? Will he be okay?"

"We may have some good news," Alfredo said. "The stage of his polio is very far along, but my friend Arturo Ferrarin is set to fly to the Pasteur Institute in Paris to fetch anti-polio serum."

"Is there not any here? Why must someone fly to Paris?"

One of the doctors spoke up. "This serum is very rare and expensive, and there's no guarantee it will work at this point; his sickness is very far along. If we'd been here days ago we may have had more options."

"How on earth did this happen?" Luciana asked. "How did he get it?"

"He spends so much time in the slums and helping the sick," Mariscia offered. "It's likely he could have contracted it from someone there, no?"

One doctor nodded, but another said, "It doesn't matter how he got it, we must focus on the serum. That's our only hope right now. All we can do now is wait."

In the passing hours, news of Pier Giorgio's sickness spread across Turin. Dozens of visitors came hoping to give their condolences and well-wishes, but Adelaide forbade all of them, even the Archbishop, from seeing her son. She feared contagion and perhaps the small possibility of a common germ being the final catalyst to his death.

"Why won't all these people leave my son alone?" she cried. "Who are they all? How do they even know him?"

A group of young Catholic students led a prayer vigil outside the home, led by Father Carlo, the priest of the

Catholic Men's Club at the Polytechnic. It seemed all of Turin sat in waiting, hoping for a miracle. But hours later a violent storm swept across the city, pounding the streets with sheets of rain and ripping the sky apart with lightning. Those amongst the prayer vigil scurried away like insects as they searched for cover.

Inside, the phone rang. On the other end of the line, a somber voice informed Alfredo Frassati that the weather would prevent any planes from taking off this evening. He hung up the line and began to cry.

33

A Final Prayer

Pier Giorgio opened his eyes. The world was hazy. A darkness hung over his room, lit up only on occasion by the flashing of lightning outside. Rain pounded against the window pane. He searched the room, seeing his family sitting in chairs around the bed. They all smiled.

"We're here with you," Luciana said quietly. "Can we get you anything?"

He shook his head. Adelaide grabbed his hand.

"Georgie, you always told us to offer up our suffering to God to atone for our sins, but I'm not sure you have any sins; won't you offer this suffering up to him on behalf of the three of us. Will you do this for us?"

"Of course," came his tired reply.

"You must let him rest," a nurse said from behind them. Her habit showed she was a religious sister as well, Sister Michelina. "I'll come find you if anything changes."

Luciana and Adelaide blew him a kiss and walked toward the door. Alfredo stood over his son, peering down at his emaciated body. He wiped at his eyes.

"I love you, son."

"I love you too, Papa."

He rubbed his head and left as well. Now alone with the nurse, Pier Giorgio said, "Sister Michelina, won't you hand me that crucifix off the wall?"

She walked toward the far wall and lifted the wooden cross off a nail, bringing it to him and placing it in his free hand; the other already held a rosary.

"Now, will you help me make the sign of the cross?"

She hesitated before slowly reaching for the hand holding his rosary. She lifted it to his head, then heart, and each shoulder as he uttered the names of the Blessed Trinity.

"Thank you, sister. Now please, could you leave me for a moment? I appreciate your care, but would like to pray in solitude."

She nodded and left the room.

And so, as the dark hours of night faded by and a storm pounded the Frassati home, Pier Giorgio began a final prayer, gripping his rosary and crucifix:

> Oh, dear Lord, won't you please forgive me for my sins? Bless me and ensure that I will rest in you in these near hours. Watch over my family, ignite them with the fire of your love, which all their life they have not felt. You must take them down the path that leads to you. Take this suffering I have endured, and through it, bring them blessings of peace. Bless my friends, whom I love so much. Ensure that they grow in faith. Oh, Blessed Mother, how I love you so. Intercede for me at this, the hour of my death. Your loving and maternal light has protected me throughout my mortal days; now, let it lead me in these final

steps to your Holy Son. Jesus, I commend to you my spirit. Your love is the cure of all. How I long to finally see you. Look not on the shadows of my soul, please, I beg of you.

Oh Jesus, meek and humble of heart, make my heart like unto thine. Oh Mary, conceived without sin, pray for us who have recourse to thee.

34
Cortège through the Streets

Alfredo and Adelaide Frassati waited for the word to be given when they could make their way outside. They sat in the den with their only remaining child, Luciana. Silence consumed them, all stunned at the rapid decline of their beloved Pier Giorgio who rested outside in an oak casket, waiting to be carried to the Church of La Crocetta.

So much became clear in the last days. He had endured the struggles of his crippling disease quietly so that care and attention would not be drawn away from the mourning of his grandmother. His humility, which should have been cherished but was ignored, had ultimately led to his demise. But his family, sitting quietly together, sat with a single acknowledgment; they had all neglected his needs, drowning in their own self-absorbed nature. Their guilt quelled their tongues from uttering his name. But if only they could read the heart of their son and brother, they would know he held no resentment toward them. Only love.

Mariscia walked into the room. "It's time."

They followed her to the front door, their heads hung low as they stepped onto the front steps. They wanted to shield their eyes from his casket.

But Mariscia spoke suddenly and with shock.

"Signor and Signora Frassati, Luciana, look . . ."

Upon raising their eyes, they saw thousands of people lining the streets. There were so many, standing in drab clothing and remaining so still and quiet their presence would be forgotten if one closed his eyes. Words escaped the family as they walked down the steps toward the horse-drawn carriage that would follow behind Pier Giorgio's casket. They climbed inside as Pier Giorgio's friends lifted him up onto their shoulders.

The procession lurched forward. As they ushered their way up the street, the mourners flooded behind them, yet still there were more with each block they passed waiting patiently to get a glimpse of the casket. Women groaned and cried as they passed by, many threw flowers before the procession, and others joined in common prayer.

"Who are all these people?" Adelaide asked her husband. "I don't understand this."

"I don't know," Alfredo replied. He was dumbfounded that he could not locate many of his friends from politics and business in the crowd. Luciana cried at the realization of how much these people loved her brother.

When they neared the church, the procession came to a halt. Alfredo helped his wife and daughter down, and together they approached the front steps, still filing behind the casket.Meanwhile, watching from within the crowd and waiting to follow the procession into the church for the funeral, stood many whose eyes dripped with tears, tears that drained from a place deep inside them. In their depths rested a wellspring which Pier Giorgio had filled with love throughout the days of his life. But he had not filled these wells by means of a powerful waterfall gushing over a mountain cliff; rather, he had filled the wells one bucket at a time. Small, virtuous acts of kindness, overlooked by the world of men, poured forth from his soul and into theirs. These acts of charity and tenderness came as constant as sunrises, lighting up their lives and warming them as they walked through a cold world. But only now, as Pier Giorgio's sun was setting below the horizon, did their eyes gaze upon the dawn of his virtues.

A young man stood watching the casket go by, about Pier Giorgio's age, with a skin disease that plagued his face and body. His name was Vincent. He had not known Pier Giorgio well, but many years ago they had shared a bowl of soup in a dark corner of a school cafeteria. Pier Giorgio had simply been his friend, perhaps his first friend, perhaps his only friend.

An elderly man, a former school custodian named Ernesto, also watched. He crossed himself as the casket passed, noting the date of Pier Giorgio's death. Pier Giorgio had been kind enough to remember his own deceased son at Mass one year after his death. In thanksgiving, Ernesto would return to this church in one year to honor Pier Giorgio.

A gardener stood with his wife. Signora Gola cried into her husband's chest. Even now she could still hear the church bells in the town of Pollone, ringing just above the shouting of Pier Giorgio's ecstatic voice as he shouted to her that her husband was coming home from war.

There also stood a soldier, beside several other wounded

veterans. Gianni Brunelli had never forgotten how Pier Giorgio begged him to come to Mass, along with his fellow soldiers. Gianni could not speak for the others, but because of Pier Giorgio he had been to Mass nearly every Sunday since returning from the war years ago.

A young man, a friend of Pier Giorgio, stood beside a sick and dying man many years in age. Pier Giorgio had introduced the two of them in 1918, and they had been friends ever since. Carlo and Signor Cavetti smiled to each other as the casket passed them, remembering their friend. Carlo, through Pier Giorgio's example, had become an ardent member of the St. Vincent de Paul Society, helping countless other men and women like Signor Cavetti.

Beside Carlo and Signor Cavetti stood another caretaker and patient. Teresa Vigna had helped a young man named Anthony sneak out of the leprosy hospital, for he would not miss Pier Giorgio's funeral. He did his best to cover up his lesions, but it mattered little, for no one looked anywhere other than the casket. Pier Giorgio had always hoped that the rest of society could look past the physical maladies of people like Anthony and see the humanity resting within them. Today, through their love of Pier Giorgio, they were not afraid to brush shoulders with a leper.

Several priests stood praying beside one another; Fr. Lombardi, who taught Pier Giorgio in grade school, Fr. Robotti, whom Pier Giorgio had served as a bodyguard for on numerous occasions, Monsignor Pinardi, who would often say Mass for the Shady Characters at the Little St. Bernard, and Fr. Righini, who'd heard Pier Giorgio's last confession, a confession that was filled sparsely with the most trivial of sins, yet from the penitent's mouth they were treated with the utmost gravity. Fr. Righini knew now why Pier Giorgio had been so adamant about receiving the sacrament of reconciliation, sitting right there in the streets of Turin. Somehow, he knew the suffering and quick demise that awaited him. And still there one was more priest—a German—Fr. Sonnenschein, whom Pier Giorgio had loved dearly. He was much older than Pier Giorgio, but something told him his young Italian friend would beat him to heaven.

Also from Germany stood a family of nine in the crowd; the Rahner family, with their seven children, each wiping at their eyes. The youngest children cried the hardest, knowing they would never see their beloved Pier Giorgio again. They longed for the days when he stayed with them in their home, warming it with his smile.

Another family cried beside them, the Costa family. Teresina and Ettore were older now, but still they bawled like young children. Their mother had overcome her sickness—she was healthy now—and she nodded toward the casket, letting Pier Giorgio know he no longer had to watch over her family. He could rest now.

Signora Converso cried the hardest of anyone. Who would come fix her broken doors? Who would bring her fresh bread from the market? Who would visit her and bring her flowers? She cried as if her own son passed in that casket.

Yet another cried as well, a woman who had held Pier Giorgio's heart in her hands, though she never knew it. Laura Hidalgo knew that she had taken her friend for granted. Never again would she see his smiling face, never again would she receive one of his letters. Her and Christina and the other female members of the Shady Characters hugged each other and wept.

Below the casket were his friends, the lives Pier Giorgio had perhaps touched the most. Upon their shoulders he rested, and within their memories he would live forever. Camillo recalled the simple nights they sat talking and smoking cigars. Marco remembered the days they spent together fighting the Fascists. Guardia, Tonino, Isidoro, and Giuseppe all recalled their adventures together, and Guido, who was present for Pier Giorgio's last mountain expedition, wished the two of them could journey just one more time toward the heights. They each lifted him up, hoping if their arms could reach high enough they could somehow repay him by sending him to heaven, though they each knew he needed no help at all.

And still there were more, members of the St. Vincent de Paul Society, the Cesare Balbo, the Third Dominican Order, the Eucharistic Crusade, the Apostolate of Prayer, and the Marian Sodality, all organizations Pier Giorgio had a tremendous impact on. Others had traveled from Germany, from the slums of Alexanderplatz, where Pier Giorgio spent nearly a year of his life serving the poor, joining alongside the sick and poor of Turin.

All these souls stood together, weeping common tears of sadness. And in that moment, two of the littlest souls sprung forth from the crowd and ran toward Mr. and Mrs. Frassati, the parents of the fallen.

"Signora!" one of them shouted. "Signora!"

Adelaide turned and watched the two young boys run toward her, dressed in rags and covered in grime. One held a rose.

"I wanted to give this to Pier Giorgio," one of them said, "but . . . are you his mother?"

She nodded.

"Then, I feel he'd want you to have it. He spoke of you often, and the rest of his family. He loved you dearly. I'll miss his visits to the orphanage. He always played games with us, and brought us treats. He was always so funny. I want to be like him when I grow up, okay?"

She took the rose. "Yes, that would be nice."

The other boy grabbed at his sleeve and pulled him back into the crowd. Adelaide began to cry. Alfredo and Luciana held her.

"How blind we were to the man our son was. How did we not see all this?" she asked through her tears.

"I don't know," Alfredo confessed.

"And what can be done now? Nothing, he's gone."

"No, Adelaide, we *can* do something. We have the rest of our lives to follow the path our son has blazed for us. He'll still be with us through all these people who loved him so much. He'll still be with us if we strive to have the faith he once had. Come, let us go inside and honor him."

He wrapped his arm around his wife and daughter and led them up the stairs, following behind the casket which held their son and brother.

And so, after many years of trying, Pier Giorgio was finally able to lead his family into church, where the presence of Christ awaited them.

Epilogue

One of the struggles that came with writing a novel about Pier Giorgio was that his life cannot be summed up in one glorious epiphany, moment or accomplishment; rather, his life was filled with a multitude of simple acts of charity and kindness. Thus, the book reads more like a collection of short stories.

In contemplating his life and the manner in which he lived each day, one might be reminded of St. Thérèse of Lisieux, the Little Flower, who stressed the importance of little virtuous deeds, knowing that through these small acts of love we grow closer to God. This truth contrasts the reality of how we drift away from God through the momentum of our "little" venial sins.

For this reason, Pier Giorgio and Thérèse are both excellent models of how we all have the ability to become Saints, despite not having any superb talents, blessings, or prestige. All we have to do is take baby steps toward God, and I assure you, He will give us the time required to reach Him. Coincidentally, both Pier Giorgio and Thérèse died at age 24, but even with their years cut short, they managed to touch millions of lives (in life and death). Meanwhile, the memories of other leaders, dictators, kings and queens fade into the shadows of history.

I attempted to convey this facet of Pier Giorgio's life, this beautiful simplicity, with the following passage, found in the last chapter:

> Meanwhile, watching from within the crowd and waiting to follow the procession into the church for the funeral, stood many whose eyes dripped with tears, tears that drained from a place deep inside them. In their depths rested a wellspring which Pier Giorgio had filled with love throughout the days of his life. But he had not filled these wells by means of a powerful waterfall gushing over a mountain cliff; rather, he had filled the wells one bucket at a time. Small, virtuous acts of kindness, overlooked by the world of men, poured forth from his soul and into theirs. These acts of charity and tenderness came as constant as sunrises, lighting up their lives and warming them as they walked through a cold world. But only now, as Pier Giorgio's sun was setting below the horizon, did their eyes gaze upon the dawn of his virtues.

The metaphor of a well being filled up one bucket at a time poetically represents how Pier Giorgio brought kindness, charity, and sanctity to everyone in his life. It was not a "waterfall" of love, just drips and drops and puddles and buckets, but even the ocean could be called a collection of drips and drops and puddles and buckets.

It's important to note too that many of his righteous deeds were overlooked. Just as with many others, and especially the Saints, he was not fully appreciated until after his death.

Thus comes perhaps the only common storyline throughout Pier Giorgio's life.

One of the first things I found amazing about Pier Giorgio when I began my research of him was that his family had such a tepid faith. How could a young man of zealous faith be raised in such a household? Where did his fire for Christ come from? It's what makes his story so unique and powerful, and so inspirational for anyone who feels sorrow over his own family's indifference to God.

Throughout his life, Pier Giorgio strove to bring his family closer to God, though for the most part he failed. His patience with them was otherworldly, something that surely tested him each and every day. At times he became frustrated, but he loved them dearly and honored and respected his parents. He never turned on them. He was loyal to the end.

I feel Pier Giorgio would be upset with me if I didn't, in closing, speak well of his family; this is what they deserve for giving him to us.

The way I have the last chapter depicted is, of course, literary license. It's not likely that his parents and sister, the very day of his funeral, had a change of heart and began to see the importance of God and their Catholic faith. However, they *were* brought to God through the death of Pier Giorgio, albeit over the course of the rest of their lives.

Alfredo, while not becoming as passionate in his faith as his son, did embark on a journey that led him back into the Church and Her Sacraments, as did Adelaide. It should also be pointed out that the two of them reconciled their marriage, making something Pier Giorgio once said to a friend seem prophetic: "I would gladly give my life if my parents would stay together."

Luciana, meanwhile, lived a long life, much of it devoted to furthering the cause of her brother's Sainthood. She wrote books and did her best to spread the word about his life. It should come as no surprise that a study of Pier Giorgio's life sparked within her a strong passion for Christ and His Church.

One may give her more room for error than her parents during those years when they all overlooked Pier Giorgio's holiness, as well as God altogether. She was young, only in her early twenties when Pier Giorgio died, and nearly all of us seem to treat God like a stranger throughout our youth. The temptation toward fun and games and anything care-free presents a difficult challenge for young people, but perhaps God understands this. We must all start out as cat-erpillars before His grace turns us into butterflies.

So considering Luciana's youth, and the simple fact that she had the same parents as Pier Giorgio, with their lukewarm faith and attraction to the glamour of high soci-ety, it's hard to hold her responsible for not being as pious and holy as her brother. Still, by the winter of her life, she became a woman who walked hand-in-hand with Christ. Without Luciana, it's possible that none of us today would know who Pier Giorgio is, and for this, I give her my own personal thanks.

And so, rather fittingly, Pier Giorgio was able to accom-plish his greatest goal. As Christ resurrected us all through His sacrifice, Pier Giorgio did the same for his family. The image of him finally leading his family into the church, but doing so in a casket, is both tragic and splendid, as tragic and splendid as the Cross.

We may not all join the ranks of Sainthood, but we can all strive to do what Pier Giorgio did, bringing our families as close to holiness as possible, and ultimately leading them to heaven. This is all God asks of us, to help each other, especially those closest to us, come to rest in Him. With the help of this young Italian, perhaps we will.

Blessed Pier Giorgio Frassati, pray for us.

Prayer for the Canonization of Pier Giorgio Frassati

"O merciful God,

Who through the perils of the world

deigned to preserve by Your grace

Your servant Pier Giorgio Frassati

pure of heart and ardent of charity,

listen, we ask You, to our prayers and,

if it is in Your designs that he be glorified by the Church,

show us Your will,

granting us the graces we ask of You,

through his intercession,

by the merits of Jesus Christ, Our Lord, Amen."